"What if I'm putting your children in danger?" Liddie asked.

"You told me yourself that someone had to have shut Daisy into the horse stall. There's no way she could have gotten in there on her own. And that note." Liddie shook her head, then pushed away from the table. "It's not safe for me to stay here."

"I'll make sure you're safe," Jonah said quietly.

Liddie looked up and they locked gazes. Standing, she tucked in the kitchen chair and braced her hands on the back of it. "It's not fair for your children. For Ellen." Liddie kept her voice low in the quiet house. "Their poor grandmother has already been through enough."

"Where would you go?" Jonah stared up at her, studying her features.

"Maybe I could call my sister."

An icy dread gathered in the pit of his stomach. "You're willing to leave the Amish? Break the rules of the *Ordnung*?"

"There's no other way."

Jonah rose, not taking his eyes off her.

"There is. You can stay here."

Alison Stone lives with her husband of more than twenty years and their four children in Western New York. Besides writing, Alison keeps busy volunteering at her children's schools, driving her girls to dance and watching her boys race motocross. Alison loves to hear from her readers at Alison@AlisonStone.com. For more information, please visit her website, alisonstone.com. She's also chatty on Twitter, @alison_stone. Find her on Facebook at Facebook.com/alisonstoneauthor.

Books by Alison Stone

Love Inspired Suspense

Plain Pursuit
Critical Diagnosis
Silver Lake Secrets
Plain Peril
High-Risk Homecoming
Plain Threats
Plain Protector
Plain Cover-Up
Plain Sanctuary
Plain Jeopardy
Plain Outsider
Seeking Amish Shelter
Amish Country Cover-Up

Visit the Author Profile page at Harlequin.com.

Amish Country Cover-Up

Alison Stone

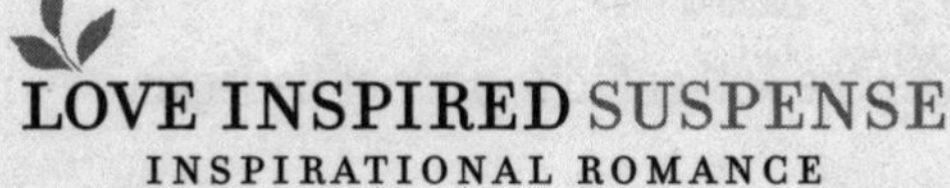

ISBN-13: 978-1-335-40520-3

Amish Country Cover-Up

This edition published by arrangement with Harlequin Books S.A.

For questions and comments about the quality of this book, please contact us at CustomerService@Harlequin.com.

Love Inspired
22 Adelaide St. West, 40th Floor
Toronto, Ontario M5H 4E3, Canada
www.Harlequin.com

Printed in U.S.A.

Trust in the Lord with all thine heart;
and lean not unto thine own understanding. In all
thy ways acknowledge him, and he shall direct thy paths.

—*Proverbs* 3:5–6

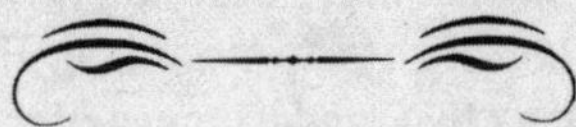

When a little voice first whispered, "Try writing fiction. It'll be fun," I was on maternity leave with my first child. So, I started on the path to publication—learning the craft of writing and the business of publishing. Now, twenty-five years later, I have almost as many books published. It hasn't always been fun (writing is hard work!), but it has been very rewarding. Thanks to my wonderfully supportive readers; my editor at Harlequin, Allison Lyons, who often has more confidence in me than I have in myself; and to my fantastic family, Scott, Scotty, Alex, Kelsey and Leah. I love you guys, always and forever.

ONE

The words on the page of the children's storybook blurred and Liddie Miller stifled a yawn. Outside the Troyers' cozy sitting room, the rain had finally stopped after falling for most of the chilly November day. She stretched her back and rolled her shoulders. Andy, the little boy tucked in next to her on the wooden bench, looked up at her with curious brown eyes—much like his *dat*'s—and asked, "What happens next?"

Liddie smiled softly at the four-year-old and placed her hand on the page. Through the wide opening to the clean but starkly-appointed kitchen, Liddie could see Andy's six-year-old sister, Daisy, sitting at the table in an apparent staring contest with her constant companion, a cloth doll. Liddie had been met by strong resistance when she tried to get the child to put it down, learning the doll had been made by her mother who had been murdered a little over a year ago. Now, the child clung to it and her grief, breaking Liddie's heart.

The steady sound of chopping suggested their grandmother was in full dinner-prep mode. Liddie knew better than to offer to help. Ellen Stoltzfus had lost her daughter and her duties as primary caregiver to her grandchildren, but she was not going to lose reign over the kitchen.

"Read!" Andy's impatient little voice snapped Liddie out of her trance.

She blinked down at the boy and let his rudeness pass. They both needed to get out of the house for a bit. "How about you and I get some fresh air?" The sun hung low in the sky, but if they hurried, she could get a break from the underlying tension that hung heavy in the air. It had only been two weeks, but Liddie was already wondering if it had been a mistake to take this nanny position. The children's grandmother resented her, and their father avoided her.

Andy scooted off the bench, his bare toes hitting the hardwood floor. "Should I get Sissy?"

"Yah." Liddie would be impressed if he could convince his big sister to join them. Andy seemed far more resilient after their devastating loss than Daisy did, and Liddie wondered if it was due to their difference in age. He was only three years old when he lost his mother. Daisy had been five. Old enough to remember. Old enough to really miss her. Shaking away the prickly cloak of heartache that seemed to smother her every time she thought about the woman she had never met, but whose children she now cared for, Liddie forced a bright smile. "Go on, ask Daisy and get your shoes and coat on. It'll be dark before long."

As expected, Daisy declined, shaking her head and staring out from behind her doll tucked against her face with her big sad eyes.

"Are you okay with Daisy?" Liddie asked the children's grandmother. "The rain stopped. Andy and I are going to stretch our legs."

"Of course," Ellen said crisply, not bothering to look up from her pile of chopped carrots. More than once Liddie had heard the older woman muttering something about having raised five children and surely, she could manage two.

"We won't be long," Liddie said cheerily, hoping eventually the older woman would warm up to her.

The pair got on their shoes, coats, scarves and gloves. The storm front had brought in a chill not unusual for a November afternoon. Liddie hoped for more warm autumn days before the cold temperatures and snow settled in for the long haul. Once that happened, she'd have to forego her early morning walks around the property where she had a chance to ponder her future. Taking care of someone else's children was only a temporary position before she found her path in life.

Liddie finished wrapping the scarf around Andy's neck and he scooted away from her and burst out the door like a bull released from its pen. His boots sloshed in a muddy puddle. She pulled the door closed and bit back a reprimand, not wanting to ruin a perfectly good outing. "Let's check on Licorice."

With that, the little boy ran ahead to the barn. "Andy, go around to the other side," Liddie called, feeling a twinge of heated discomfort spread up from under her scarf. Licorice's stall was on the far side of the barn, opposite from where his father kept a woodworking shop.

In his enthusiasm, Andy tugged on the door, letting out a little groan of frustration when it didn't budge.

"Come on, let's go around to Licorice's stall." Liddie reached for Andy's hand when the door swung open, revealing the boy's father, specks of sanding dust peppering his dark beard.

"I'm sorry, we didn't mean to disturb you. We wanted to check on Licorice." Liddie found herself babbling.

"I'm going to feed Licorice," Andy said, his constant movement propelling him into his father's woodworking shop. The little boy's tiny hand ran across the arm of a rocking chair, perhaps mimicking something he had seen his father do.

"Of course." Jonah Troyer blinked slowly, tracking his son's movements. It seemed as if he had just woken from a nap, or perhaps he had been absorbed in his work. The sweet smell of freshly-sanded wood mingled with manure. Jonah had transformed half of the barn into a tidy woodworking shop where he seemed to retreat to avoid his family. Or maybe it was her he had been avoiding. In the short time she had been here, she didn't have enough information to decide. The only one who spoke less than this man was his sweet daughter.

A clatter drew her attention to the little boy who had knocked over a broom. "Be careful," she cautioned.

Andy righted the broom and continued his zigzagging around a workbench and a toolbox. He peeled back the sliding door that separated one space from another. Licorice's stall was on the other side of the divider.

"Excuse me," she said to Jonah, and hustled to catch up to the energetic little boy. By the time she reached the horse's stall, Andy had torn off his gloves and was holding out his flat palm, feeding the horse a carrot. A pile of carrots sat on an overturned bucket outside the stall.

"Can we take him out and let him run?" Andy asked.

Liddie considered this a moment. She was more than capable. She used to hitch up her own horse, Brownie, to the buggy, and offer to run every possible errand her family might need. She loved the freedom. However,

Jonah had insisted that her only job here was to take care of the children. "We should probably ask your *dat* first." An ember of annoyance flickered in her belly. Had she moved out of her father's house—with his strict rules and accusatory gaze—only to have to ask permission to do something as simple as exercise the horse?

Jonah's your boss, a quiet reminder whispered in her head. *And isn't it the Amish way for women to ask permission?*

Liddie shook away the nagging reminder, knowing full well that every relationship was different. Even her *dat* who seemed so upset with her lately deferred to her *mem* on certain matters. Liddie pinched the string of her bonnet and twisted it around her gloved finger. She missed her horse. And she missed her family. Even though they all lived in Hickory Lane, without transportation they might as well be miles and miles away.

"Another time, okay? It's getting late." Liddie ran her hand down the horse's soft mane. "How would you like that, old girl? Maybe we could take a ride into town." She cooed at the horse. It certainly would break up the long days, especially as the weather got colder.

"We could get candy at the grocery checkout like *Mem* used to let us." Andy smiled brightly, his baby front teeth slightly crooked, and he grabbed another carrot and fed it to Licorice. If the thought of his *mem* made him sad, he didn't show it.

Liddie touched Andy's shoulder when he reached for yet another carrot. "That's probably enough for now. Should we take a walk?"

Andy wiped his slobbery palm on the side of his pant leg and turned to her. "Can we play catch?" Without waiting for an answer, he ran through the opening to his father's workshop. He grabbed a baseball mitt from one of the benches. Jonah didn't lift his head from whatever he was doing. Liddie had never played baseball before, but she couldn't refuse the little boy.

Andy pressed a mitt into her side. "Here, you can use my *dat*'s."

At the mention of his name, Jonah lifted his gaze. Liddie felt her face heat when their eyes connected, but the moment was over in a heartbeat. Jonah poured something on a rag and ran it over the freshly sanded wood. A pungent chemical odor filled the space.

Liddie turned her back to her boss and accepted the soft leather mitt from her charge. She peeled off her winter gloves and set them on the bench. She stretched her fingers to fit into the grooves that were better suited for Jonah's large hands. Strange how she was taking care of this man's children, living inside his home with the children's grandmother, yet she barely knew him.

Andy ran outside and Liddie was relieved to follow. A stiff wind bent the tall vegetation that had taken over the untended farm. She pulled her thick black bonnet lower over her ears and a shudder skittered up her spine. Looming over the purple loosestrife and ragweed plants was the ominous greenhouse in need of some serious TLC. She found herself averting her gaze, as if she didn't see it, it didn't exist, nor did its history. Jonah's wife, Maggie, had been murdered inside the building after surprising a drugged-out vagrant. A weight settled on Liddie's chest as she struggled to imagine what Maggie must have experienced in her final moments. The fear. The terror. Did she know she was going to die?

"You stand there," Andy said, forcing Liddie out of her head and into the moment. He pointed to a spot and used his outdoor voice to tell her to back up, back up, *back up*.

"If I go any farther, I'll end up in the weeds."

Andy giggled. "Can you catch?"

"I'll try." Liddie glanced over at the barn door to make sure Jonah wasn't watching them. She wasn't up for making a fool of herself, yet the thought that he'd bother to come and watch was ridiculous. The man was completely absorbed in his work, whether it be his construction jobs away from the farm or his woodworking at home.

Turning her attention back to Andy, Liddie held out her glove and scrunched up her face. The little boy cocked his arm and released the ball in a wild throw, sending it flying over her head and into the weeds.

"You missed it!" Andy shouted in glee. Liddie couldn't help but laugh, but then immediately sobered at the thought of tramping through the weeds toward the greenhouse to retrieve his errant throw.

"Stay here while I get it." Liddie tossed Jonah's mitt on the ground and parted the weeds, dodging the prickly ones. The cloying smell of cigarette smoke reached her nose and she froze. Did Jonah smoke? It seemed unlikely. The muffled crunch of dead weeds soaked with rain sounded nearby. Heart thundering in her ears, she called through a dried throat, "Hello? Is someone there?"

The footsteps ceased, but the unmistakable scent of cigarette smoke still lingered.

Liddie glanced over her shoulder. Andy stood in the clearing, oblivious to her, throwing his glove up into the air and letting it land with a thud. She turned back toward the greenhouse. Then her eye was drawn upward to a flock of geese overhead, their persistent honking drowning out her ragged breath. She reached out and bent the sturdy stem of a dried weed and peered toward the greenhouse, the structure in heavy shadows as dusk gathered around them. She took another step and reached a small clearing in front of the abandoned structure.

"Hello?" she called again. Curiosity had her moving toward the greenhouse when someone exploded from around the corner and slammed into her. A scream ripped from her throat as her elbow, then her hip slammed into the wet, hard-packed earth, knocking the wind out of her.

Straightening, Jonah pressed his hands into the small of his back and stretched. He had spent a long day in his workshop and didn't foresee quitting anytime soon. He never thought he'd feel like a stranger in his own home, but that's what hiring the pretty young nanny had done to him. Simply appreciating that she was attractive made him uneasy. Hadn't *Gott* already blessed him with his one and only true love? Whom he lost when she was murdered because he wasn't here to protect her.

He would never forgive himself.

Jonah picked up the piece of sandpaper and folded it over, looking for a fresh patch of grit. He let out a long sigh, recalling the pure joy on Andy's face when he grabbed his baseball mitt and asked Liddie to play with him. When was the last time Jonah had played with his son?

Dismissing his thoughts, he leaned over and ran the sandpaper over the rough edge of the wood. A scream ripped through the *scratch-scratch-scratch* of the steady back-and-forth motion of the sanding.

He froze and straightened, unsure of what he had heard. His pulse roared in his ears, and all the tools hanging in neat rows along the wall shifted into sharp contrast as his vision tunneled.

"Dat! Dat! Dat!" His son's panicked screams set Jonah's blood running cold. Instinctively, he grabbed the hunting shotgun from behind a cabinet and bolted out of the barn toward the cries of his son.

Andy stood by the edge of the weeds, his eyes wide with fear, tears streaming down his cheeks. When had it gotten so dark?

"What's wrong?" Jonah forced out the words from a too-tight throat. The weight of his gun gave him little reassurance under his sweaty palms. He followed Andy's gaze. "Did Liddie go into the greenhouse?" No one had gone in there since Maggie…

Jonah shook away nightmarish images that flooded his brain. "Where did Liddie go?" The question came out harsher than he had intended. His young son's lower lip quivered as he failed to form any words. Jonah tamped down his mounting anxiety, afraid he'd scare his son into silence.

"Andy," Jonah said more calmly this time, "where's your nanny?"

His son lifted his trembling hand and pointed toward the greenhouse. A band of grief and apprehension squeezed Jonah's lungs and made it hard to draw in a breath. *Don't just stand there. Help her.*

"I threw the ball into the weeds." His son's soft voice sounded like it was coming from the far end of a long tunnel. "Liddie went to get it and she screamed." His little nose flared. "She told me to stay here when she went to get the ball." His sweet boy. The rule follower.

"Okay." Jonah placed a firm hand on his son's thin shoulder. "Run back to the house. Don't come out until I come get you."

Andy spun on his oversize rain boots and bolted toward the house. Jonah then stepped into the weeds. The roaring in his ears drowned out his own breathing. The crickets. Geese in the distance. He blinked a few times, struggling to adjust to the darkness that had blanketed the farm, transforming the weeds and the structures into amorphous shapes.

He stomped through the weeds, wincing as a sharp thorn dragged across the flesh on the back of his hand. A sliver of the moon shone high above the greenhouse. He made his way toward the small clearing in front of the run-down structure and called out her name, then after no answer, louder. "Liddie? Liddie?"

Jonah's eyes were drawn to the greenhouse door. He reached out with a shaky hand for the handle, his mind's eye flashing back to the day he witnessed his wife's lifeless body splayed across the ground. He had arrived at the same time as the rescue vehicles.

Everyone had been too late.

He had been too late.

He pushed the door open, then he heard a sound behind him. He spun around, lifting his gun.

Muffled cries drifted across the field, prickling the hairs on his forearms. Charging toward the sound, he froze when his eyes adjusted to the dark and he discovered two figures struggling. Someone seemed to be dragging Liddie across the field. He ran toward them, then paused. Holding his breath, he steadied his aim at the unmistakable outline of a man. "Let her go."

The man pushed Liddie, and she hurtled toward him. Jonah lowered the shotgun and reached out with his free arm to stop her forward momentum. The person took off across the field, disappearing into the overgrown vegetation.

Jonah steadied Liddie, holding her at arm's length, then he dropped his hand. The moonlight reflected in her eyes. "Are you okay?"

"Yah, yah..." she whispered, her voice shaking.

"Who was that?"

"I don't know." Liddie turned toward the barn, her perfect profile outlined in the soft light of the early evening sky. Her eyes seemed to flare, then she took a quick step and stumbled. "Andy. Is Andy okay?"

"*Yah*, he's in the house." Jonah steadied Liddie by gingerly taking her elbow. "Let's get you out of the cold and call the sheriff's department."

As much as Jonah hated to deal with law enforcement, he didn't have a choice. He couldn't be responsible for another murder on his property.

TWO

Jonah guided Liddie to his woodworking shop where he called the sheriff's department with a cell phone he kept for business purposes. When he ended the call, he stopped and carefully studied Liddie pacing the small space, her delicate hand by her face.

"Are you sure you're okay?" he asked, suddenly hyperaware of his surroundings, of her.

Liddie cut him a sideways glance and nodded, seemingly reluctant to say anything.

"Did you know that person?"

Her gaze went wide and she jerked her head back, as if he had offended her.

"I mean, do..." He let his words trail off. What did he mean? He suddenly felt guilty that he had been avoiding her for the most part since she came to live here to work as his children's nanny. He had thought engaging her in conversation, treating her as part of his family, would somehow make him disloyal to his wife's memory. Now, he realized it only served to put a distance between them that now was going to be tough to bridge.

"A deputy should be here soon." He eyed her coat,

now muddy from being dragged across the field. "Are you warm enough? Maybe we should go in the house."

Liddie stopped pacing and crossed her arms tightly over her chest. "I'm fine."

A small kerosene heater hissed in the corner of the workshop. He hadn't been this protective of someone other than his children in a long time. For some reason, he felt responsible that a stranger had dragged his children's nanny across his field. Just like he had felt responsible for his wife's death. He hadn't been there when she was attacked because he had been working construction in the suburbs of Buffalo. A small whisper of gratitude skittered across his brain. Thank *Gott* he had been home today. That he had heard his son's screams.

Inwardly he shuddered at the alternative.

What was going on? Why was *Gott* testing him so?

Jonah moved to the open barn door where he could watch for the deputy and keep an eye on his home where his children were with their grandmother. "Perhaps it would be better if we stayed here to talk to the deputy in private," he said. "I don't want to scare the children."

Liddie nodded.

A few minutes later, a sheriff's patrol car turned onto his property. His mind flashed to another time when his farm was overrun with patrol cars and rescue vehicles. The workshop suddenly felt close and the floor swayed. He ran his hand nervously down his beard and stepped out into the yard to get some air. He sensed Liddie following him, but he didn't turn around to check. Even though it was dark, he didn't trust that his expression wouldn't betray his feelings. Feelings he had kept stuffed down inside for the past thirteen months for the benefit of his children. He needed to be strong for them. And it was easier to suppress his emotions than air them in the light of day.

Deputy Eddie Banks climbed out of his car and strolled over to them. “Hello, Jonah.” The man’s stern gaze, lit by the soft light flowing from the workshop, turned to Liddie. “Hel-lo.” He stretched the single word into two long syllables that sounded more like a question than a greeting.

“This is Liddie Miller,” Jonah said, not giving her an opportunity to speak for herself. “She’s my children’s nanny. Someone grabbed her by the greenhouse.” Saying the words out loud sent renewed fears skittering up his spine. Had whoever killed his wife returned?

He took off his hat and scrubbed a hand across his hair. *No, no, no.* That wasn’t possible. That man had been arrested and sadly killed himself at the county lockup.

The deputy adjusted his stance, hooking his thumbs on either side of his utility belt. “Perhaps you can tell me what happened, Miss Miller.” The way he pronounced *Miss* sounded like a swarm of angry bees.

“Of course.” Her voice sounded softer than usual. “Andy and I were tossing a ball around and when I went to retrieve it from the weeds, I smelled cigarette smoke. When I called out, someone attacked me and then dragged me across the field.” Liddie touched her forearm, as if remembering where he had grabbed her.

“Did you recognize them?”

“Neh,” Liddie said, and a faraway look descended into her eyes, as if she were reliving the moment. “It was dark. He had a hood on.” She seemed to be choosing her words carefully. “He might have had a scarf. I can’t…”

"It's okay." The deputy turned his attention to Jonah. "Did you get a look at him?"

"Like Liddie said, it was dark, and he had his face concealed."

"Okay." The deputy seemed to be considering something. "Jonah and I will take a look around the property. Why don't we see you safely to the house, *Mizzz* Miller?" That buzzing sound again. It struck him as condescending.

Liddie looked like she wanted to say something more, but she simply nodded.

Jonah escorted her to the house, checked on his children and mother-in-law, then met the deputy in the yard. The deputy directed his flashlight in the direction of the greenhouse. "Seems you've had a run of bad luck on this farm."

Jonah didn't bother to respond.

As they walked through the field, the beam of light danced over the weeds, lighting occasionally on the greenhouse, then back to the earth. After they were convinced the man was no longer on the property, they headed toward the house. "I'll patrol the area. See if anyone's lurking," the deputy said.

"I appreciate it." Jonah didn't know whether to be relieved or disappointed that they didn't find anyone.

The deputy took a step toward his patrol car, then turned around. "I know it's none of my business, but how well do you know your nanny?"

"Liddie?" Jonah asked, confused. "She was recommended by her grandfather who is a friend of the bishop's." He hadn't felt the need to explore the details of her life beyond that.

"You've had a lot of hardship, Jonah, and I'd hate to

think this young woman brought something from the outside world that is better left out there." He lifted his palm to the generic "out there." His choice of words reflected his job of enforcing the laws among a group of people who had a strained relationship with the sheriff's department. The Amish preferred to remain separate.

Jonah's blood chugged slowly through his veins like molasses, as his mouth went dry, his mind raced with all the possibilities. "What has Liddie done?"

Liddie kicked off her muddy shoes in the aptly named mudroom. She slid off her coat and hung it over the edge of the utility sink. Clumps of mud clung to the hem of her dress.

"What happened out there?" Ellen appeared in the doorway, clutching the apron of her dress. "Andy is beside himself. He said Jonah had to save you."

"I'm fine." Liddie searched behind the older woman for the young boy. "Where's Andy?"

"He's curled up on the bench with Daisy. He's had a terrible fright."

Daisy. Thankfully the shell-shocked little girl hadn't witnessed the attack.

"I'll tell you more later, but right now I want to check on Andy."

Without saying a word, Ellen moved to one side of the doorway. She found Andy exactly where Ellen said he would be. Liddie crouched down in front of the boy, her weighted hem dragging on the hardwood floor. She smiled warmly at Daisy who stared blankly back at her before Liddie turned her focus back to Andy. "Are you okay?"

The little boy immediately sat upright and nodded

and started talking excitedly with a touch of awe. "Why were you yelling? I called for *Dat*. Did the bad guys try to hurt you, too?"

Liddie placed her hand on his knee. "You did a *gut* job. Your daddy was a big help. I'm perfectly fine." She and Jonah hadn't discussed what they'd share with the children, so she made a decision on the spot to keep things vague and upbeat. "Your daddy is talking to the sheriff's deputy and he'll be in shortly."

"Did someone try to hurt you? Are they going to arrest him?" Andy hopped down from the bench and raced to the window and peered out. Liddie's attention drifted to Daisy, who watched her brother with the same air of concern that always wafted off of her. Poor child.

"Everything's okay," Liddie repeated for Daisy's benefit. "No need to worry." Tell that to the unease weighing heavily on her chest.

Liddie wandered over to join Andy. The deputy was talking to Jonah and they both kept glancing toward the house. Based on the prickling at the base of her neck, she suspected they were talking about her.

Liddie touched Andy's head. "Come away from the window."

"Can you read to me?" Thankfully, he had forgotten that she never answered all of his questions. She didn't want to scare him.

"Of course, but I want to talk to your *dat* first, okay?"

"Okay." Andy picked up a Matchbox car from a nearby basket and drove it along a hardwood plank, as if the lines were the edges of the road. Daisy watched from behind her doll.

"I'll read to both of you," Liddie said, mustering up as much enthusiasm as she could.

Who had attacked her? Gingerly she touched her forearm, feeling the start of a bruise from where his fingers dug into her arm.

Liddie stepped away from the window as Jonah turned to walk toward the house with a somber expression. Once inside, his primary concern was his children. "Everyone okay in here?" The smile strained his face as he reassured his children. "Everything is perfectly fine, okay? Daddy's always going to make sure you're safe." Liddie sensed that was a promise he vowed to keep. Then, Jonah turned toward Liddie. "Can we talk in private?" He pinned her with an intense gaze that made her stomach flip. Was she in trouble? He held out his hand, guiding her toward the kitchen.

Ellen appeared in the doorway. "I can put dinner out for you two. I already fed the children, although they didn't eat much. Andy usually has a better appetite." Liddie sensed the children's grandmother was searching for the information neither she nor Jonah had been willing to share.

"*Denki*, Ellen. But I'd like to talk to Liddie. Maybe in a little bit."

"Okay then." The older woman's posture deflated.

Apparently sensing his mother-in-law's worry, Jonah added, "Ellen, everything is going to be fine. *Ich bin dankbar.*" *I am grateful.*

Ellen nodded. "I'll read to the children."

Jonah waited a beat until his mother-in-law had retreated to the other room. He hesitated another moment until Ellen's thin voice floated into the kitchen as she read a well-loved story. Liddie and Jonah settled in at the kitchen table.

He placed his folded hands on the table, leaning slightly toward her. "Are you okay?"

"I'm fine." Anxiety heated her face. "Tell me, what did the deputy say? Did you find anything?"

"*Neh*, whoever attacked you is long gone."

Liddie sighed heavily. "Oh…"

"Did you know who it was?" His narrowed gaze did nothing to ease the sting of the question.

"I already told you…" She couldn't help but bristle at the accusation. Like her father's pointed questions about how she was responsible for leading a kidnapper to her sister's doorstep. "What did Deputy Banks say about me?"

"He told me about your involvement with some—" he cut a glance toward the sitting room as if to make sure little ears weren't listening and Liddie couldn't help but to fidget with her dress, suddenly eager to get into warm, dry clothes "—drug dealers."

Liddie's mouth went dry and any words of defense got lodged in her throat. "That wasn't my fault. I…" Her thoughts swirled; she didn't want to sound like she was making excuses. She cleared her throat and tried again, keeping her voice low. "When I visited Bridget, my sister, during my *Rumspringa*, I met a guy by the pool in her apartment complex." She tapped her fingers on her thigh, thinking, thinking, thinking. *Neh*, she needed to go back and explain from the beginning for this to make sense.

None of this makes sense.

Liddie plowed forward before she lost her nerve. "At the time I visited Bridget, she was in nursing school. She also worked at a health care clinic and had reported her concerns that her employer, a doctor, was illegally prescribing drugs." Even as she retold the story, it felt surreal. "The doctor had been involved with some very bad people who were determined to silence my sister." Liddie drew in a deep breath to quell a familiar queasiness that washed over her. Surprisingly, her stomach rumbled at the smell of fresh-baked bread. She almost forgot she hadn't eaten dinner. She shook away the thought. "This guy I met by the pool was part of a gang distributing the drugs. I had no idea." She disliked how naive this all made her sound.

"Deputy Banks said you had kept in touch with him, leading him to Hickory Lane."

"I did." Tears burned the back of her eyes and she looked up at the ceiling to keep them from falling. "I'll never forgive myself. I had no idea. I misjudged him. But thankfully, Bridget's okay. She's married to the DEA agent who saved her. They now live in the Virginia area. All the people involved have been arrested."

Jonah's knuckles grew white as he clenched his hands in front of him. "How can you be sure?"

Liddie ran a shaky hand over her forehead and heat crept up her neck. "What are you saying?" Her voice cracked over the last word.

Jonah flattened his work-worn hands and ran them back and forth across the surface of the table, as if he were carefully considering his words. Something about the gesture made her wonder if he had crafted this table himself. "My children are the most important thing to me."

"The children are important to me, too." She straightened her back and leaned toward him. "I'd never let anything happen to them."

"Sometimes things are out of our control."

"Are you letting me go?" She hated the tremble in her voice, but she couldn't help it.

The pitter-patter of feet drew their attention to the entryway to the kitchen. Andy ran over and threw his arms around Liddie's shoulders.

Steeling herself, Liddie smoothed her hand over his soft hair. He smelled of fresh air and little boy sweat. "Now, now. What's wrong, sweetheart?" Glancing up, she found Jonah staring at her. She couldn't read the expression in his eyes.

Andy lifted his tearstained face. "Are you going to leave us like my *mem*?"

"I…um…" There was no way she could lie to this child. Not after everything he'd been through.

But what's the right answer?

Liddie looked to his father for help. Her pulse whooshed-whooshed-whooshed through her ears like the tension-filled seconds ticking away between them.

Jonah finally blinked and his hard expression softened. He pushed away from the table and came around to her side and crouched down in front of his son. He drew him away from Liddie and took his hands in his. "No need to worry, little man. Liddie's not going anywhere." Then he met her gaze. "She's welcome to stay as long as she likes."

THREE

The next morning, Jonah woke as the first hint of dawn colored the sky in shades of pink and purple. The morning air was cool as he strode out to his barn with a new sense of purpose. As a kid, he used to enjoy the early mornings, doing his chores, building up a good appetite, then running in to have a big plate of his *mem*'s golden-fried scrapple with apple butter. The vivid memory made his stomach rumble.

Jonah had left his home in Apple Creek when his wife's parents could no longer tend the huge farm. However, months after they arrived, his father-in-law passed and an opportunity for Jonah to work construction in nearby Buffalo proved to be a steadier means of income. It seemed like a logical decision.

However, time away from the farm, meant time away. He hadn't been home to protect his wife. Now, after the recent attack on his nanny, he would not stand idly by while Outsiders thought his abandoned greenhouse was a good place to hang out and get high.

Why was his farm such an attraction? Was it truly because he had allowed the greenhouse to fall into a state of disrepair and had abandoned the land his in-laws had tended for sixty-some years?

Nimmi! No more!

Jonah ignored the whisper of guilt and collected a few tools from his workshop and strode down a small path that wound behind the barn to the greenhouse, defying the weeds' efforts to consume it. His jaw ached from clenching it. He had avoided coming anywhere near the place of his wife's murder. On his trips back and forth from the barn, he tended to avert his gaze, unable to see the bare wood and clouded glass rising above the out-of-control weeds without being overwhelmed. Drawing on his anger and grief—his constant companions—he hefted up the sledgehammer, adjusting his gloved hands on the smooth wood of the handle, and slammed it down, carelessly crashing through a window. Glass rained down in a glittery mess.

Jonah leaned back on his heels and groaned loudly. Gingerly, he picked out a shard of glass from the back of his leather glove. Perhaps his need to destroy the greenhouse would allow him to vent his frustration, but he'd have an awful mess to clean up. Maybe there was a better way to take this structure down, perhaps reuse the materials.

Footsteps sounded behind him and he spun around. His son emerged from the path, his eyes bright with excitement. An immense sense of love warmed Jonah's heart. The cowlick in the boy's part was reminiscent of his own unruly hair that was more pronounced when he took off his hat after a long, sweaty day working construction.

"I couldn't keep him inside." Jonah's gaze traveled up to Liddie's. She had an apologetic look in her eyes. "Ellen told us you were going to tear down the greenhouse and Andy begged to come see. It's such a nice morning. I hope you don't mind."

Jonah removed a glove and tousled his son's hair. "I suppose a wrecking crew is hard to resist for a four-year-old." He stepped forward, the glass crunching under his boot. He definitely needed to take a more organized approach to tearing this down, otherwise he'd have to risk one of his children cutting themselves on glass or a stray nail.

Jonah locked gazes with Liddie. "Can you take him back to the house to get proper gloves? We have a lot of work to do."

If Jonah hadn't been watching Liddie's face, he would have missed the flicker of a smile on her pink lips. Guilt sloshed in his gut. He had been too hard on her, allowing himself to listen to the rumors that tarnished a good woman's name so recklessly shared by the deputy. Hadn't they all made mistakes in the past? Hadn't the bishop recommended her? Next chance when they were alone, he'd reassure her that the nanny job was hers as long as she'd have it, and he wasn't just saying that while they sat around the kitchen to appease his son.

"Can I look for my baseball first?" Andy asked.

Jonah glanced at Liddie, then down at his son. *"Yah."*

Andy took off in a crouched position into the nearby patch of weeds. Liddie approached Jonah with a look of concern. For some reason, his apology died on his lips.

"I talked to my brother-in-law late last night," Liddie said, keeping her voice low so as not to be overheard by his son. "The DEA agent," she added for clarity.

A ticking started in Jonah's jaw, a reflex almost. Perhaps he had been too quick to give her a pass if she thought it was acceptable to break the rules of the *Ordnung* in his home. "You have a phone?" The question came out hard and clipped.

Liddie's face colored. "*Yah*, I have a cell phone tucked in the bottom of my wardrobe. I promise I don't use it unless I absolutely have to." She paused a moment, then said, "I guess it's my security blanket, much like your daughter's doll."

He searched her face, and despite himself, his heart went out to her. She obviously was struggling with her place and perhaps this phone was her quick ticket out of here if she needed it. Could he have it on his conscience if he was the one who finally pushed her to leave the Amish? Didn't he have a responsibility to encourage her to stay? He nodded his silent understanding. "What did you learn?" They needed to have this conversation before his son emerged from the weeds with his ball.

"Zach assured me that all the parties involved with my sister's kidnapping are incarcerated." Her wary gaze scanned the field where she had been dragged last night. What would have happened if he hadn't been close? If he had been away on a construction job in Buffalo? He shoved the thought away.

"That's good to know." All of this was so far out of his depth, yet he was beginning to wonder if *Gott* had brought them on the same path for some reason. Maybe helping Liddie was part of his penance for not being there for his deceased wife. He scrubbed his bare hand across his face, then stuffed it back into his leather glove.

Liddie flattened her lips, as if struggling to find the words. "Is there any chance the person who hurt… I mean..." No one liked to use the word *murdered*, he understood that.

Jonah shook his head slowly. "He was arrested and died by suicide in jail." Then, to stop her from playing any more guessing games, he added, "Deputy Banks assured me that his fingerprints were on..." Now he found himself groping for the right words to describe the bloody weapon, a metal pipe that had once been the innocuous support for a plant stand. His poor wife hadn't stood a chance.

"I don't understand." Liddie drew up her shoulders and a shudder seemed to course through her despite the relatively warm morning sun beating down on them. It seemed she shared a similar fear: what if yet another outside evil had crept into their midst? How random. How daunting. How would that even be possible?

"Got it!" Andy popped out of the patch of weeds holding his baseball aloft, dispelling the thick tension with a jubilant smile of victory. "Can we play, *Dat*?"

"Perhaps after we do some work. Would you like to help?"

His son nodded excitedly, immediately making Jonah feel bad about how he had been running away from everything this past year—his pain, his home and his family.

"Perhaps Daisy would like to come out and help, too," Jonah suggested. "We could start with carrying all the flowerpots and items out of the greenhouse and store them in the barn. Maybe we could sell them at the upcoming auction where they're raising money for Daisy's classroom." The idea of finally tackling this long overdue task made his nerves hum.

The concern creasing the corners of Liddie's blue

eyes had been replaced by a lightness he didn't recognize. She normally watched him with wariness or caution, probably because he made it difficult for her to know what to expect from him. His behavior had been downright rude, yet he still couldn't shake the idea that kindness toward this woman would be a betrayal of sorts. As if by punishing her, he was punishing himself.

Jonah needed to find a way to settle his thoughts. To find peace. It was not *Gott*'s will that he would be weighed down by excessive burdens, but rather be set free. He needed to dig deep. Rely on the same faith that had gotten him through the worst year in his life. Taking action to remove this eyesore would be a positive step in dissuading any other squatters.

Protecting his family.

A sense of purpose warmed his heart on the gorgeous autumn morning. His children were healthy, and this pretty young woman brought a much-needed change into their home that had been swamped with grief. She deserved his acceptance for the blessings she had brought his children.

Jonah tilted his face to the sun and for the first time since that fateful day when his world had tipped on its axis, he felt a flicker of hope. Of what life, with *Gott*'s blessing, might look like on the other side of pain and suffering.

It felt wonderful to get outside and do something productive. Liddie had missed working on her family's farm, the fresh air, the sun beating down on her, aching muscles. Lately, the only muscle that ached was her backside from sitting too long, reading the children stories or watching them quietly play. Her role—for better or worse—was to keep an eye on the children. Period. Ellen held such tight reins on the house, as if it were her last domain.

Today, Liddie's job was to help the children clear out the greenhouse. Daisy seemed content taking the lighter flowerpots from her brother at the door and carrying them with one hand to a Radio Flyer wagon on the worn path. She dragged her dolly along in the other hand. She never stepped into the greenhouse, as if some invisible force stopped her short. Liddie couldn't imagine the horror the child had seen when she found her *mem* unresponsive and bloodied on the ground inside the greenhouse. Her grandfather had shared that bit of information when he told her about the nanny position. This knowledge allowed her to be ever patient in trying to draw the quiet girl out of her shell. A task at which she had yet to be successful.

"You're doing such a good job, Daisy." Liddie smiled brightly and was rewarded with the tiniest of smiles on the sweet child's face.

"Maybe the girls can pull the wagon and unload the flowerpots in the barn. Stack them in the corner of my workshop." Jonah seemed in his element working here, his sleeves rolled up, revealing tanned forearms. He had been home more the past few days. She suspected the construction jobs were winding down with the anticipation of the coming winter.

"Of course we can," Liddie said, admiring how Jonah involved both his children. She crouched down to Daisy's eye level when she didn't answer. "Do you want to pull? Maybe your dolly can ride in the back." Liddie cleared out a spot for the doll and Daisy hesitated a moment, before nestling the doll in a clean spot between the stacks of clay pots.

The little girl picked up the handle and tugged, but couldn't move the wagon. Liddie reached out and grabbed the neck of the handle, freeing one of the front wheels from a divot. Daisy pulled the wagon and Liddie walked close by to prevent the pots from tipping over. The child took instruction well and went inside the barn and began unloading. Liddie noticed the girl mouthing numbers, "One, two, three..." as she stacked the mud-caked pots. Liddie couldn't help but smile to herself.

"*Dat* needs a crowbar." Andy ran into the barn with his usual enthusiasm. "It's on the back wall. That's where he said to look. You can reach it. But I get to carry it to *Dat*." Jonah's son spun around, repeating, no doubt, what his father had told him. His bright eyes took in all the tools on all the walls as he searched for the prized crowbar.

"Hold on. Let me look." Liddie scanned the back wall and found what she suspected Jonah needed. She stretched and plucked it off the hook. She was surprised by the solid weight of it. She handed it to Andy. The metal bar was almost as long as he was. "Got it?"

Andy held up the bar and smiled. He ran outside through the back door closest to the greenhouse and Liddie heard a yelp. She glanced over at Daisy, still diligently stacking the pots. A cross breeze blew in from one open door to another. "I'm going to check on your brother. I'll be right back."

The little girl kept up her job. A few feet from the barn door, Liddie found Andy bent over, studying his pant leg. The crowbar rested on the ground nearby.

"What happened?" she asked, tilting her head to try to see what had him engrossed.

Andy straightened, a frown pulling on his chapped lips. "I tripped and ripped my pants."

Liddie was about to reassure him, tell him she could mend his pants, but she knew better. "Your grandmother can fix that."

"She's going to be mad. She told me to be more careful."

Compassion tugged at her heartstrings. This little boy had enough going on in his life without worrying about an innocent mishap.

"Well, if she's too busy, I can do it." Liddie snapped her fingers. "Just like that."

"Really? I've never seen you sew."

Liddie laughed. "Trust me, I know how to fix tiny holes. Your pants will be good as new."

She picked up the crowbar. "Can I carry this to your father for you?"

Andy nodded, some of the enthusiasm from earlier drained out of him. Poor guy.

When they reached the greenhouse, Jonah had the door off its hinges. He turned to her and his brown eyes felt warm and welcoming. Was she supposed to notice such things about her boss? She blinked, feeling her cheeks warm, and she looked down at Andy. She handed him the crowbar. "Here you go."

Andy stretched out his hand, took the crowbar and in turn, offered the tool to his father triumphantly.

"Looks like you guys are all set." Liddie turned on her heel and went back to the barn. When she entered the workshop rich with smells of freshly sanded and stained wood, something immediately felt off. The stillness sent goose bumps racing across her flesh.

"Daisy?" The little girl was nowhere to be seen. Her knees grew weak and her vision tunneled. *Deep breath. Relax.*

Liddie stepped farther into the workshop and found a stack of flowerpots tipped over. Others were smashed with the force of someone slamming them onto the ground.

"Daisy," Liddie called again, struggling to hear her own voice over the thundering heartbeat in her ears.

Liddie rushed to the other open barn door, convinced she'd find the little girl in the yard. That's when she saw it: Daisy's favorite dolly, lying on the ground, one leg dipped in a muddy puddle. Liddie ran over and snatched it up, upset on Daisy's behalf that her precious doll had been discarded.

The morning sun dimmed and Liddie thought she was going to be sick. Daisy would have never left her doll here. "Daisy," she called again, this time louder.

No answer.

With adrenaline heightening her senses, Liddie bolted to the house, hoping to find Daisy there. Of course she went to the house. Where else would she have gone?

Liddie found Ellen sitting in the rocking chair, working on her latest knitting project. "Did Daisy come back inside?"

"No, she was with you." The elderly woman's accusatory tone cut through her, then her gaze dropped to the doll in her hand. Ellen lowered her needles and a worried expression replaced the flash of annoyance. "Is something wrong?"

Not wanting to alarm Ellen, Liddie tried to explain. "She must have gotten past me on the way to help her *dat*."

The children's grandmother peppered her with questions as Liddie pulled the door shut. Clutching the doll to her apron, Liddie sprinted to the greenhouse. Her pounding steps jarred her entire frame, exacerbating her throbbing headache. The entire way, she hoped—prayed—she'd run into Daisy with big fat tears over her lost doll.

When Liddie reached Jonah, he and his son were pressing down on the handle of the crowbar. A father teaching his son how to pry off a wood slat. A father-son moment about to be shattered.

Jonah released his grip and straightened. All the color drained from his face. "What is it?"

"I can't find Daisy."

FOUR

I can't find Daisy. Liddie's words pinged around Jonah's brain. His knees nearly buckled and he planted his hand on the rough wood of the greenhouse frame above Andy's head. His son's face was scrunched up as he pushed down on the crowbar with all his might. "Come on, *Dat*. Help!"

"Hold up, buddy," Jonah said, as if on autopilot as he scanned the path behind Liddie, willing his sweet little girl to appear. When she didn't, he reached down and unhooked the crowbar from under the slat and tossed it down on the grass and pivoted to face Liddie. "Isn't she in the barn?" He ran the back of his hand across his sweaty forehead, pushing his felt hat back a fraction.

The desperate look in Liddie's blue eyes was a jab to the heart. His pulse whooshed in his ears and a shadow crossed the landscape.

"She's not in the barn or the house." Liddie's lower lip quivered. The confirmation that they had a very real problem dangled in her raised hand: his daughter's favorite doll. "I found this in a puddle outside of the barn." A look of fear flashed in the depths of her eyes. "There's no way she would have left this behind."

Jonah's gaze drifted to the field where Liddie had been attacked and dragged last night. Had the assailant come back and abducted his daughter? A band tightened around his lungs, making it difficult to breathe.

"*Dat*, we have work to do," Andy said, bending down to scoop up the crowbar. Jonah watched absentmindedly as his son pressed the edge of the crowbar against the greenhouse.

"We need to search all the outbuildings." Liddie's urgent command snapped him out of his shock.

"We'll work on the greenhouse later." Jonah grabbed Andy's hand and tossed the crowbar away again, keeping his frustration in check. "We have to find Sissy now." He forced a light-hearted tone despite the fact that his heart was about to explode out of his chest.

His son tugged his hand free and crouched down to grab the crowbar again. Jonah bit back a scolding. Impatience and panic warred for dominance.

Liddie held out her hand and Andy readily took it, apparently sensing his father's swell of emotion, but unable to pinpoint its source. "We can work on that later," Liddie said. "I need your father to help me find your sister."

Something in her tone had his young son squinting up at her in the bright sun. Confusion swept across his face. "Where did Sissy go?"

"I don't know." Liddie led his son toward the barn. The child had to run to keep up with her frantic pace as she double-checked inside his workshop and the stalls. "Do you and Daisy ever play hide-and-seek? Is there someplace she might hide? Somewhere outside?"

Andy shook his head. "*Neh*, we're not allowed to play outside because *Mammi* can't keep up with us." His mother-in-law had always preferred quiet, indoor activities. That had been part of the appeal of hiring a nanny.

Jonah swung back the door separating his workshop from the rest of the barn. They searched around, behind, between. The little girl was nowhere to be found.

"Okay…" Liddie seemed to be considering something, but Jonah was growing impatient.

Why had he let his guard down and allowed the children to play outside, especially while he was trying to work? Especially after last night? But he had been right here. Liddie had been right here. He bit back the blame resting on his lips.

"Take Andy to the house and stay there," Jonah said, not bothering to hide his agitation. "I need to find Daisy." He planted his hands on his hips and debated the most likely places she'd go if she had wandered off on her own.

He trusted Liddie to take his son to the house while he circled back around the barn. Where could Daisy have gone? The last time—that he knew—she ventured away was when she found her mother's body. Even since, she had been hesitant to wander beyond the front porch. Today had been a huge milestone, watching her work industriously packing up the flowerpots.

Jonah took his hat off and ran a shaky hand through his hair. Why was this happening? Was *Gott* punishing him for something?

"Daisy!" he called, his voice ringing across the fields. "Daisy!"

Jonah went through the barn again with no sign of her. Since he hadn't noticed her come by the greenhouse, he suspected she might have gone the other way toward the neighbors'. *Yah*, he thought to himself.

Maybe she had wandered over to visit Amity, their teenage neighbor who frequently visited their farm. A ray of hope allowed him to catch his breath.

"Daisy!" he called again as he ran over to the Beilers' farm through a worn path that separated the two properties.

The eerie quiet made his nerves hum. His eyes darted around the yard. No sign of any of their five children. *That can't be good.* Jonah marched toward the house, hoping the children could help him search. Or maybe his daughter had been welcomed inside for a visit, however unlikely.

Please, please, please, let Daisy be okay.

Jonah remembered pleading with *Gott* when the paramedics loaded his wife into the ambulance. A prayer that had gone unanswered. A prayer that was already too late.

He let out a long slow breath as his panic started to spiral out of control.

Once he reached the porch, he turned around, cupped his hands around his mouth and hollered, "Daisy!"

The door creaked open behind Jonah and he spun around. Amity Beiler emerged from the house, the strings of her bonnet flapping in the breeze. "What's wrong, Mr. Troyer?" She held her coat tight around her.

"Daisy's gone missing."

A line creased her forehead. "Wasn't Liddie watching her?"

Jonah disregarded the comment. "Have you seen her? Maybe one of your siblings…?" His pulse whooshed in his ears, every beat another second ticking away.

"My family went into town to deliver the pies. I stayed behind to clean the kitchen." She tapped the toe of her boot on the dry-rotted wood of the back stoop, the casual gesture seeming to belie any sense of urgency. Maggie used to complain that the girl always got underfoot when she came to visit, making it take longer to prepare dinner or hang the laundry. The only reason his deceased wife never sent her away was because she felt sorry for her. She seemed lost in her own family.

Jonah stepped off the porch. "Come help me find her." He tossed a glance over his shoulder.

Amity's eyes grew wide. "Of course."

Jonah planted his hands on his hips and called his daughter's name again. As he got closer to the Beilers' barn, he heard dogs yelping. "I'm going to check inside." He knew how much Daisy loved the puppies.

Amity lifted her shoulders a fraction. "I'll look with you."

Jonah nodded, then spun around to the barn. He tapped the rusty latch on the heavy door. His flicker of hope extinguished as he considered how unlikely it would have been for his young daughter to manipulate the catch. He swung open the door, the bottom dragging across the mud. A puppy bounded out, nearly tumbling down the slight incline. Amity scooped up the puppy and followed him into the barn.

Jonah blinked a few times until his eyes adjusted to the shadows interrupted by lines of sunlight threading through the slats. Heart beating wildly, he moved down the row of stalls, checking each one.

Empty.

Empty.

Help me find Daisy. Please.

Jonah reached the last stall, the only occupied one. The horse neighed in greeting, shaking its mane. He was about to admit defeat when a piece of purple fabric poking out from under the door caught his eye. He let out a long breath he hadn't realized he'd been holding. He swung open the stall door, sidestepped a startled horse and fell down on his knees next to his precious daughter.

"Daisy!" He checked her dirty face with his hands. His eyes. He had to convince himself she was okay.

She was okay. *Yah*, she was okay.

Thank You, Gott.

"How did you get in here?"

Daisy shrugged. A fuzzy white puppy peered up from the hammock made from the fabric of her skirt stretched over her crossed legs.

"I see you found a friend."

Daisy's gaze went behind him to Amity, who lingered outside the stall. "Oh dear, she's going to need a bath," the teenager said, unhelpfully.

Jonah angled his daughter's face to study her uncertain eyes when immense relief washed over him. "Are you okay?"

Daisy blinked and a tear tracked a light line down her dirt-stained face. "I want to go home."

Clutching Daisy's doll to her chest, Liddie paced the front porch, her gaze scanning the farmland around her. A growing ache thrummed in her heart. She had been hired to do one job. Only one job.

And she had failed.

"Oh, Daisy, where are you?" Her mind flashed back to the man's rough fingers digging into her forearms, dragging her across the field. What if that man had come back for the little girl?

But why?

She paced, needing to expend some of her pent-up energy. She quelled the instinct to call the sheriff's department, praying Daisy had just wandered off and Jonah would be back with her momentarily. *Please, let that be the case.* Tears burned the back of her eyes, but she refused to cry.

The door creaked behind her and she spun around. Andy stuck out his head. "Did *Dat* find Sissy?"

"Not yet." Liddie steeled her voice so that the little boy wouldn't detect her fear.

"Come back in here," Ellen called from inside, her sharp tone indicative of her fear. "You need to stay inside *with me*." Liddie couldn't help but feel that the emphasis on the last two words were for her benefit. And she deserved it. Liddie feared these children would grow terrified of anything beyond their four walls.

"Go on," Liddie said, encouraging Andy to obey his grandmother. She didn't want him standing outside if his father came back without his sister. He'd be distraught. They'd have to call the sheriff's department. Then what…?

She released a long, slow breath. Nothing good would happen if she started panicking. She drew in a deep breath, then out. A prickling dread rolled up her neck. The deep breathing wasn't working. Her mind raced. How had she become a magnet for really awful things? What if they couldn't find Daisy? How could she bear it? How could any of them?

She shook the thought away. Think good thoughts. She resisted her childhood training to pray at such times because she felt like she'd be a hypocrite. Her father had asked her more than once to get down on bended knee, ask for forgiveness and be baptized. But her conflicted feelings for the future had led to a stalemate. When, or if, she decided to be baptized in the Amish community, it had to be her decision.

Not her father's.

Now here she was, employed as a nanny because she wasn't welcome in her own home because she wasn't ready to accept all the tenets of her faith. Yet, she wasn't ready to completely abandon them either. She drifted between the beliefs of her childhood and the uncertainty of her future.

Lacking in faith was a lonely place to be.

An approaching car on the country road drew her attention. She half expected to see a patrol car pull up the lane. When a pickup truck whizzed past, she groaned. "Where are you, Daisy?" If the child wasn't found soon, they'd need help. Time was precious.

Liddie started scanning the land again, willing Jonah and Daisy to appear. Needing to fill the void, she drew in a deep breath and finally mumbled an uncertain prayer, "*Gott*, I know I haven't followed the *Ordnung*, but…" She shook her head, and started over. At times like this, she had to shed man's ways and focus on *Gott*'s. Dig deep and find faith. "Watch over Daisy and bring her home." The simple prayer brought her a sliver of peace.

She braced her hand on the railing and bowed her head. "Please bring Daisy home safely."

A yelping sounded across the field. It sounded like one of the Beilers' puppies. She squinted in that direction. First a white fur ball bounded out from behind the weeds, then Amity. Liddie gritted her teeth. She didn't feel like dealing with their chatty neighbor right now, then she mentally scolded herself. Hadn't she herself once been the misfit trying to find her place? Running to Buffalo on *Rumspringa* to visit her sister? Courting trouble. She thought at age twenty-four she'd be settled down by now. More accepting of others. Maybe Liddie still was that misfit.

A breeze fluttered the fabric of Liddie's dress that poked out from under her long black coat. A chill raced up her spine. Wouldn't Amity have run into Jonah since he was searching for Daisy on her family's farm?

Liddie stepped off the porch to approach the teenager, when Jonah appeared carrying Daisy. Her knees grew weak with relief. She dropped the doll on the porch step, then rushed to yank open the door to tell Andy and Ellen the good news. "Jonah has her. Jonah has Daisy."

Not waiting for them to respond, Liddie raced down the porch steps, across the lawn. Before she reached Jonah, Amity said, in almost a world-weary way, "She was in the barn playing with one of the puppies."

Liddie cut the teenager a sideways glance and rushed up to Jonah. She placed a hand on Daisy's back. The girl lifted her head. "Where did you go?" Liddie's gaze slid from Daisy to her father. A muscle twitched in his jaw and he gave a slight shake of his head.

Liddie followed them onto the porch. When he reached for the door, Amity called out. "Want me to put the puppy in the barn?"

"Ah..." Jonah seemed to hesitate and Liddie wasn't sure what was going on. "Here." He reached out and took the puppy in his free hand and held it against his chest next to Daisy. *"Denki."*

"If you need anything else," Amity offered eagerly.

"We're going to get Daisy cleaned up," Liddie said plainly, eager to get inside with Daisy and Jonah.

Amity's cheeks colored and Liddie immediately regretted her dismissive tone. She forced a tight smile, a feeble effort to soften the blow since Amity clearly intuited she wasn't welcome. Not right now, anyway.

"I'll see you later," Amity called to them as they slipped inside.

Liddie waved. "Bye." She closed the door behind her and sagged against it. Jonah set the puppy down and it seemed to struggle to gain purchase on the hardwood floor. He then carried Daisy over to the bench where they shared their storybooks. Liddie had so many questions for Jonah. Where did he find Daisy? Was she okay?

Before she had a chance to ask, Andy rushed over and knelt down, putting his face against the puppy's. "We got a puppy?" Their new pet seemed happy to have all the attention if his wagging tail was any indicator.

Meanwhile, Jonah was crouched in front of his daughter, his hands placed on either side of her. "You cannot run off. You had us worried."

"Where did you find her?" Liddie asked.

"She was in a stall on the Beilers' property. I can't figure how she got herself in there." Worry creased the corners of his eyes. He gently touched Daisy's knee. "Can't you tell me how you got in there?" He had obviously asked her this previously. Daisy dipped her head, seemingly closing in on herself.

Ellen came over and touched the girl's cheek. "You got yourself into some trouble, didn't you? And it seems your father forgot he was a child once. Perhaps he'll give you a pass today. You're usually such a *gut* girl."

Daisy's grandmother smiled despite her watery eyes and held out her palm to the puppy. "Seems like you found a new friend. It's clear to me she wandered over to visit this little guy." She raised an eyebrow. "I'll go make some hot cocoa." Ellen turned and smiled at Liddie. "Hot cocoa for a cool fall day." Liddie smiled in return, so grateful Daisy was okay.

Daisy remained silent despite all the fuss being made over her. She hugged her legs to her chest, resting the heels of her muddy boots on the edge of the bench. It was then that Liddie remembered the doll she had dropped on the porch. She grabbed it, and came back in. Hard mud on the fabric crumbled under her touch. "I'll get your dolly cleaned up. She'll be as good as new." Liddie's heart felt a million times lighter with the little girl's return.

Daisy held out her arms for the doll and Liddie handed it over, mud and all, when something fell from it. Jonah reached down and picked it up. Liddie's stomach dropped. She studied Jonah's face as he unfolded the piece of paper. His grew red. Without saying anything, he handed the note to Liddie.

Run, Liddie, run.

She looked up, locking gazes with Jonah. Her face burned with shame, embarrassment, fear. She couldn't pinpoint the emotion. Had she unwittingly led someone to his farm? To endanger his children?

"Do you have any idea what this means?" Jonah asked, his steely gaze hard to read.

"Neh, neh..." The note was written in juvenile handwriting, but that didn't mean much. She lowered her voice so only he could hear. "The bad people I knew

are in jail." Jonah closed his fist around the note in Liddie's hand.

"*Dat*, are we going to keep the puppy?" Andy's question popped the tension-filled moment.

Jonah blinked a few times, then looked down at his son. A sad smile turned the corners of his lips. "Would you like that?"

"Yah!" Andy scooped up the dog and it yelped.

"Careful, little man," Jonah said, taking the dog from the eager child's arms. "Let's let him explore. Get used to the place. We'll have to find some blankets for a bed and we'll have to round up a water bowl. Lots of things to make a nice home for him."

It seemed Jonah was shifting his focus to something he could control. The serious conversation would have to wait. So, Liddie turned her attention to his daughter who was picking dried dirt from her doll. "I can wash that for you," she offered tentatively, doubtful the girl would hand over her most prized possession.

Daisy nodded and offered up the doll her mother had made for her. Liddie's heart swelled. She'd take the wins wherever she could get them. And having Daisy safely home and opening up—even just a fraction—was a huge win.

She'd deal with the note, and Jonah, later.

FIVE

A sliver of moonlight streamed in through the bedroom window, lighting on Jonah's precious sleeping daughter. Her new puppy was curled up on the foot of the bed, his leg twitching in his puppy dreams. Jonah leaned over and ran a hand down the animal's soft fur and couldn't help but smile. Customarily, Jonah would have never allowed a pet in the house, but the puppy seemed to provide his daughter some solace. For the first time since her mother's passing, Daisy didn't have her doll pressed to her face as she drifted off to sleep. He gently touched her head. What happened? he wondered. Daisy refused to say how she ended up in the neighbor's barn. Amity claimed she hadn't seen anything either. A nagging dread threatened to spoil his sense of gratitude. His daughter was safe.

Quietly he stood and the puppy lifted his head momentarily to make sure his new master was safe, then settled back in. Jonah crept downstairs. A soft light glowed in the kitchen and he found Liddie sitting at the kitchen table with two cups in front of her. She looked up when he entered the room. "I made you some tea."

She pushed back and stood. "It might be cold. I could warm it up for you."

Jonah held up his palm. "It's fine. Please. Sit."

He pulled out a chair across from hers, careful to lift the legs so the scraping noise wouldn't wake the sleeping household. It was obvious they both had today's incident on their minds. They hadn't had much time to discuss the note that fell from Daisy's doll. Instead of calling the sheriff's department once again, Jonah took it upon himself to double-check the barn, the greenhouse and a small shed on the property. None of them were occupied. Then he secured the locks on the doors that had been installed after his wife's murder.

Is this what life had become?

Liddie was the first to speak. "We've discussed this before, but I feel I need to insist on leaving."

Jonah knew she could leave on her own accord, but for some reason, she was seeking his permission. It was obvious she was conflicted, despite her urging. He took a sip of his lukewarm tea, mostly to gather his thoughts. Then he set it down and folded his hands on the table in front of him. "Is there something you're not telling me?"

A pretty pink hue colored her cheeks in the soft lighting. He hadn't meant to make her uncomfortable, but he had to get to the bottom of this. "*Neh*, I shared my unfortunate experience with some *Englischers* after visiting my sister. My sister's husband has assured me the guilty parties are in jail." She released a long shuddering breath. She glanced toward the window, a faraway look in her eyes, then she met his gaze. Something fluttered in their depths. "The reason I took this job was because my father and I weren't getting along." She turned away again, as if the admission shamed her. The Amish had a way of doing that to people who didn't toe the line. Guilt them into compliance. Jonah understood the reasoning. They felt it was for the greater good. For the salvation of their very soul.

"My sister's kidnapping," Liddie continued in a soft voice that felt intimate in the dimly lit room, "and the subsequent breakup of a notorious gang in Buffalo was big news. However, one of the biggest angles of the story was the fact that me and my sister are Amish. My sister continued her nursing studies in Buffalo, while I came home." Liddie pressed the back of her hand to her mouth, then let it drop. "News trucks were parked outside my family's farm, taking videos, trying to get interviews. My father blamed me for all the unwanted attention." She dipped her head, and one of the strings of her white bonnet fell forward. "He was right. It was all my fault. I'm ashamed. I thought I was so grown up. If I hadn't kept in touch with the person I considered a friend from Buffalo, the gang would have never tracked us down to Hickory Lane."

"We all make mistakes." His stomach ached with the thought of all the mistakes he had made. "What happened to the Amish tenet of forgiveness?" he mused out loud.

"Oh, my father is a good man. A *Gott*-fearing man." Liddie immediately went into defensive mode. Honor thy father and mother was also important. "I think his reaction came more from fear. He had already lost Bridget and he felt the outside world encroaching on his. I'm not sure his coolness toward me was intended to get me to leave, but rather repent. I overheard him telling my mother once that he hadn't been strict enough with Bridget. That it had been his fault they lost her.

That is their shame." She shook her head, then rubbed her forehead. "It's all so complicated, isn't it?"

Jonah wanted to extend his hand across the table to cover hers, but resisted. It wouldn't be appropriate. He cleared his throat. "The bishop and your grandfather are *gut* friends. I trust that the bishop would not have recommended you watch my children if he..." He let his words trail off. Who was he to judge? Who were any of them to judge? *Judge not, that ye be not judged.* How many times had he read those words in the gospel of Matthew?

"I appreciate the sentiment, but what if I'm putting your children in danger? You told me yourself that someone had to have shut Daisy into the horse stall. There's no way she could have gotten in there on her own."

"Daisy refuses to talk much since her mother's death." Familiar regret ate away at his gut. "I want to believe she wandered over to see the puppies." He left the "but" unsaid.

"It doesn't make sense that she would have dropped her precious doll. And someone smashed the flowerpots. And the note." Liddie had obviously been rehashing today's events, too. She shook her head, then pushed away from the table. "I don't know what happened, but it's not safe for me to stay here."

"I'll make sure the children are safe. I'll make sure you're safe." If only he could have done the same for Maggie.

Liddie looked up and they locked gazes. Standing, she tucked in the kitchen chair and braced her hands on the back of it. "It's not fair for your children. For Ellen."

Liddie kept her voice low in the quiet house. “Their poor grandmother has already been through enough.”

“Where would you go?” Jonah stared up at her, studying her features.

“Maybe I could call my sister.”

An icy dread gathered in the pit of his stomach. “You’re willing to leave the Amish? Break the rules of the *Ordnung*?”

“There’s no other way.”

Jonah rose, not taking his eyes off her. “There is. You can stay here.”

The next morning, Liddie woke up and tugged the covers over her head as the events of the past few days crashed over her. What she wouldn’t give to wake up with only thoughts of breakfast on her mind. Instead, regret and worry pressed on her heart, and a persistent buzz of apprehension made her wary of what the new day would bring.

Pushing aside her concerns, she got ready for the day and hurried downstairs. Ellen was already in the kitchen and the fragrant smell of apple pancakes reached her nose. A feeling of nostalgia caught her off guard. She missed home. Her *mem*. Her little brothers. Her big sister. But the life she yearned for no longer existed. Her sister had jumped the fence. Soon her brothers would find wives and start families of their own. Everyone was growing up. Moving on.

Would she ever be able to move past all the poor choices she had made? Find her place in this world?

“Good morning,” Liddie said more cheerily than she felt as she stepped into the kitchen. “Can I help you with anything?”

Ellen lifted the spatula and shook her head. *"Neh, neh..."* The two simple words came out on a sigh, sounding more weary than usual.

"I'll get the children up."

Liddie turned to leave when Ellen added, "We don't keep animals in the house."

Liddie turned back around. "We never kept pets in the house either. They always had the run of the farm and a nice cozy bed in the barn."

A flicker of a smile touched their grandmother's lips, as if she were surprised they could find common ground over such a simple thing. "Daisy seems to be attached to the puppy," the older woman mused, turning back to her pancakes bubbling in the cast iron pan.

"Yah." Liddie had crept upstairs last night to check on Daisy and her heart had been warmed when she found Jonah petting the dog as it lay curled up on the bottom of her bed. Liddie had slipped away unnoticed, feeling like she had invaded a private, vulnerable moment.

"Make sure the puppy does his business outside." Ellen squared her shoulders. "I keep a clean house."

She felt a certain lightness in her limbs. "The children and I will make sure of it. He might be a nice distraction."

"You've decided? You're staying?" Ellen continued to tend to the pancakes.

Liddie jerked her head back and a warm flush heated her cheeks. Had Ellen overheard her discussion with Jonah last night? Despite his invitation to stay on, she hadn't answered him. He had advised her to sleep on it. And she had. She didn't want to leave, but she was still conflicted about putting Daisy and Andy in further jeopardy. From what or whom she had no idea. Maybe her father had been right in suggesting all the news coverage from her sister's kidnapping would continue to invite bad things into their world. Her world.

"I—" Before she had a chance to answer, the puppy started barking at the top of the stairs. "Uh, I better get him outside."

"Go, go." Ellen waved the spatula at her. "I'm going to burn the children's breakfast."

Liddie climbed the stairs and scooped up the puppy. Daisy appeared in her bedroom door in her PJs, lines from her pillow on her face. "Did you sleep well?"

Daisy nodded.

"Have you come up with a name for this little guy?"

"Snowball because he's white and fluffy. Like snow," Daisy said, her voice soft but clear, surprising Liddie since the child's replies were usually short mutterings of the *yah* or *neh* variety.

Liddie couldn't contain a smile. "Let's get Snowball outside so he doesn't have an accident."

A tiny smile flickered across the child's face.

When they reached the bottom landing, Ellen said, "Let Jonah know breakfast is almost ready. He's in the barn. Sold a few more rockers. Someone's supposed to pick them up this morning."

"Sure." Liddie pulled open the door and the bright early-morning sun hit her face. She stepped back inside and pulled a quilt from a rack and wrapped it around Daisy's shoulders. "This will do for the short time we're outside. You can stay on the porch with your stocking feet."

Liddie carried the puppy down the porch steps and set Snowball on the grass. The puppy sniffed around the edge of the porch. Liddie returned to the porch and encouraged Daisy to sit in the rocker. She adjusted the quilt tightly around the child. "Here, tuck your feet in." Daisy bent her legs and draped the blanket over her stocking feet. "Now you'll stay nice and warm."

"Denki," Daisy said.

Loud voices sounded from across the yard. Jonah was standing by a red van talking to another Amish man, no doubt the person who had purchased his handiwork. After a short discussion, the two went into the barn and came back with the rocker. When they couldn't open the back doors of the van, the driver climbed out. The *Englischer* adjusted his pants and strolled around back. Liddie's attention turned to Daisy who was staring, wide-eyed, at the man.

"Is something wrong?" Liddie asked as pinpricks blanketed her scalp.

Daisy didn't answer, but her gaze was transfixed. A strange energy charged the air.

Jonah and the Amish man loaded up the rocking chair and slammed the back doors shut. The driver climbed in behind the wheel. Liddie suddenly recognized him from her *Rumspringa* years, when she used to go to *Amisch-Englisch* parties. His name was Dean something. She couldn't quite remember. He must have felt their stares, because he turned to study them as he drove past, lifting his hand in a mock salute.

All the color had drained from Daisy's face and her body began to tremble. Something was definitely wrong.

"You can talk to me, Daisy. What has you so frightened?" A steady pulse ticked in Liddie's ears, making her feel dizzy. She picked up the puppy and placed him gently in Daisy's lap, eager to comfort the child. The fur ball licked Daisy's chin, then she bowed her head and buried her face in his fur. She muttered something unintelligible.

"What did you say?" Liddie's breath caught. "Tell me again. It's okay," she cajoled.

"That man hurt my *mem*."

SIX

Jonah watched the van pull out onto the country road with one of his rocking chairs in the back. His Amish roots told him to be humble, yet he couldn't help but be proud that others held value in something he had made with his own two hands. It was a different kind of feeling than the sense of accomplishment that left him conflicted after a hard day's work at a construction site of a fancy home. The people who lived in those homes insisted on three-car garages for two cars. Four bedrooms and they had only one baby. Ornate kitchens where he suspected no one cooked. The life of excess was beyond comprehension. But the steady paycheck kept him coming back despite the fact that he hated leaving his children to earn it.

Shoving the thought aside, Jonah tucked the money from the sale of the rocking chair into his toolbox and locked it away. When he emerged from the barn, he saw Liddie crouched down in front of his daughter. The familiar hum of unease crept up his spine. Would his family ever find peace?

When Jonah reached the porch, he could hear Liddie's soothing words to his daughter.

"Is something wrong?" he asked, stepping onto the porch.

Liddie looked up at him, her eyes filled with worry and concern. She turned her attention back to Daisy. "Can you tell your *dat* what you just told me?"

The little girl ran her hand down the puppy's back. Her new pet seemed more than content to stay in her lap.

"Please," Jonah said.

Wrapped in the quilt with Snowball curled up on her legs, Daisy struggled to get out of the rocker.

"Here." Liddie scooped up the puppy and set him down.

Daisy flung off the quilt and stood. "I want to go inside." Thankfully, his daughter appeared to be opening up since Liddie's arrival, but she still seemed frightened of everything. She pulled open the screen door, ushered the puppy in, then let the door slam in its frame, leaving Jonah and Liddie outside alone.

"Tell me what's going on," Jonah said pointedly, hating the harshness of his tone. One thing he had learned this past year was that fear manifested outwardly as anger. He couldn't help himself. All the warm and fuzzy feelings of earlier today drained out of him, leaving him with a constant buzz of anger and dread.

Liddie straightened and drew in a deep breath. She turned to him and said, "How well do you know that man?"

Jonah's brow furrowed as he glanced toward the barn, then back at her. "Levi Jacobs? He lives in the community. His wife is due a baby soon. I sold him one of my rocking chairs." What was she getting at?

"*Neh*, not the Amish man. The man driving the van." Liddie's eyes sparked with something he couldn't quite identify. "Do you know Dean...?" She pressed her fingers to her temple and furrowed her brow in concentration. "I can't remember his last name."

"I don't know that man." Most Amish hired the occasional driver, but Jonah had never met that particular one. He rubbed the back of his neck, trying to recall if Levi had mentioned his name, but was coming up blank. A ticking started in his head, much like it did when his life was about to implode. He wasn't sure how much more a simple, *Gott*-fearing man could take. He suspected he was about to find out.

"When Daisy saw that man, she said..." Liddie's voice cracked as she seemed to be carefully picking her words "...she said that he hurt her *mem*."

Heat exploded in his chest and he shook his head in disbelief. "That's not possible."

Liddie drew up her shoulders. "I'm only repeating what she said."

The roaring in Jonah's head grew louder. "You're mistaken." He shrugged to contain his anger and he took a step toward the door. "I need to talk to Daisy. Assure her that she's wrong." His voice held a hard edge no matter how he tried to calm himself.

"Hold on. Let's talk a minute first."

Jonah froze and lifted his palm, silently inviting her to continue.

"Daisy discovered her mother after she was...well... when she died?" Her voice softened as she grappled to frame the question. Liddie cleared her throat and looked beseechingly at him. "Is it possible that Daisy saw the murderer?"

Jonah took off his felt hat and ran his hand over his hair. "Daisy found her mother, but she did *not* witness her…" Now it was he who couldn't bring himself to say the word.

"What did Daisy say about that day?" Then, apparently recognizing the insensitivity of the question, she reached out and touched his arm in comfort, only briefly, before pulling it away. Pink splotches blossomed on the smooth skin of her cheeks. "I'm sorry. I'd never pry…"

Jonah wanted to tell her it was okay. Most people avoided the mention of his wife. Her name. Her murder. As if sidestepping the most crushing moment of his life would bring him less pain. As if the mention of it, of her, would suddenly remind him of something that already occupied his every waking thought. As if he needed a reminder. It was absurd.

Now, a year after Maggie's death, his primary goal was navigating the grief. For him. For his two children. And it seemed Daisy needed the most help since she was imagining things.

"You didn't pry. Come walk with me." Jonah turned and stepped off the porch and away from the house because he didn't want his children to overhear. He paused and cleared his throat, struck by the empathy openly displayed on her pretty features. "Daisy has never said anything about that day. Absolutely nothing."

Liddie's warm eyes narrowed imperceptibly. "Never?"

Jonah shook his head, feeling a familiar tightening in his chest. "Not after she told her grandmother that her *mem* wouldn't wake up. It's like she shut down after that."

"I know this is hard for you, but we have to talk about this. What happened the day Daisy's mother died?" Liddie asked, her voice floating over him as his mind drifted back to that day, the day he had returned from work to find the emergency vehicles on his property. When he was led back to the greenhouse. Then to watch his wife being loaded into an ambulance.

A technicality.

She was already dead.

Jonah scratched his forehead, then dropped his hand and took a deep breath. "I wasn't home that day." He turned and stared off into the distance, afraid that if he made eye contact with Liddie, she'd see into his dark soul, the guilt and regrets. "Later, when I talked to Ellen, she told me that Daisy had gone out looking for her mother. When she came back, she was hysterical. She said her *mem* was hurt and wouldn't wake up." He allowed his gaze to land on Liddie's face. Tears shimmered in her pretty blue eyes.

"Is there a chance that Daisy did see the murderer?"

"*Neh*, definitely not." He tried to sound confident, but a creeping doubt began to take shape. No way. Not possible. "She was traumatized. She's confused. She saw her mother lying on the ground in the greenhouse." He glanced toward the house where he imagined his daughter was sitting in a rocker next to her grandmother, holding her dolly or petting her new puppy. His uncertainty grew, invading his account of the events. "If she saw the person, she never said anything."

"What if she did see something but was too scared to say anything? Or what if, because of the trauma, she didn't remember until she saw him today?" Liddie's hand gestures became animated. "I'd see him at parties back when I used to do that sort of thing. He was bad news then." The pace of her speech quickened as she worked to put the pieces together.

Nothing about this situation fit neatly into place. "*Neh*, it wasn't this man. I am certain. They found fingerprints. They arrested him." Oliver Applegate. He'd never forget that name.

Liddie tilted her head and made another stab at his account of the events. "What if there was more than one person in the greenhouse that day?"

"Applegate could have accused someone else. He didn't." A throbbing started in Jonah's head. *What if? What if? What if?* He dragged a shaky hand across his beard. "No, the man responsible was arrested and killed himself in jail. End of story."

Liddie wrapped her coat tighter around her midsection and glanced back at the house. No sign of the children. No listening ears. She turned back around and studied Jonah. The anguish on his face was palpable. "I don't know why your daughter seems to think she recognized that man, but you can't dismiss her." Daisy was only six, but Liddie knew what it was like not to have her father in her corner. And how horrible it was to feel like she was on the outside looking in with nowhere to go. "Maybe this is just the beginning. Maybe she'll finally start talking and tell us what exactly happened yesterday when she went missing."

Jonah's eyebrows shot up. "Did she accuse this man of locking her in the stall?"

"*Neh, neh.* I'm only suggesting that we need to create a safe space for Daisy to talk."

Jonah seemed to consider this a moment, then gave a sharp shake of his head. "My daughter did *not* witness her mother's murder." Despite the crack in his voice, he was adamant. Liddie wasn't sure if his comment was simply pure denial, or he hadn't told her everything about the day of his wife's murder. Perhaps he believed he was shielding his daughter from interrogation. Maybe this was why Daisy hadn't spoken much over the past year. Perhaps it had to do with not only finding her mother bloodied and unconscious, but also witnessing the violent act that took her life.

Liddie pushed back the queasiness roiling in her belly. "Is there something you're not telling me about the day Daisy found her mother?"

Jonah's gaze hardened and something sparked in his eyes. Anger? "*Neh*, my daughter did not see the person who took her mother away. Do not bring my daughter into this again."

"I didn't mean to cause you pain." Liddie cleared her throat. "We need to call the sheriff's department and report this, at the very least." She wasn't sure how she had allowed him to talk her out of it yesterday after Daisy disappeared.

"Oliver Applegate's fingerprints were found on the metal pipe..." Jonah got choked up and turned his back to her briefly. She bit back a second apology. They needed to have this discussion. She needed to know why Daisy thought Dean had hurt her mother. She clasped her hands, waiting for him to continue.

"They got the guy," Jonah said, matter-of-factly. "The outside evil that murdered my wife is dead. He killed himself in jail." The words spilled out, as if he were trying to convince himself. "Deputy Banks has assured me of that more than once. We have to stop drawing attention to our farm." He lifted his hand to the barn and the greenhouse beyond. "You saw firsthand what curiosity by Outsiders did to your family. I experienced it, too. I don't want a repeat of camera crews. Reporters. My children have suffered enough trauma. I can't help but think the constant focus has made Daisy see things where there is nothing to see. She doesn't know many Outsiders. She heard a bad guy hurt her *mem.* And here comes an Outsider and she equates him with that bad man." His shoulders sagged as he seemed to be thinking out loud. Reasoning things away.

A band tightened around Liddie's lungs. She had barely followed the horrific news of a murder in Hickory Lane. Of course, word of Maggie Troyer's death had spread to her farm, but Liddie had been so absorbed in her own turmoil, she intentionally tuned out the details, other than to know that after an arrest no one in the greater community was in danger. She had been in self-preservation mode back then. She feared if she read the papers, she'd find a photo of herself taken with the long lens of a camera by someone eager to capture the Amish girl who had been unwittingly involved with a Buffalo gang. Her cheeks grew hot with the familiar heat of shame. She had naively believed the outside world would go away if she ignored it.

Instead, the worst of what lingered just beyond the Amish community kept finding her.

Wasn't that what Jonah was trying to do now? Ignore it and hope it went away?

"The driver of the van was always in trouble," Liddie persisted. "What if he was with this Applegate person?" She had to keep posing the question no matter how many times Jonah insisted it couldn't be true.

Jonah sighed heavily. "Deputy Banks is just going to reassure me. I'm not going to call him." The finality of his statement made Liddie's heart sink. She sensed he disliked Deputy Banks's dismissive nature as much as she had. The Amish wanting to stay separate didn't always work in their favor, especially when they needed law enforcement. Like now.

"I have an idea." She broached the topic carefully. "I met another deputy over this past year. Deputy Elizabeth King. Believe it or not, she's former Amish." Jonah jerked his head back in surprise. "*Yah*, go figure.

"She was very helpful after I returned to Hickory Lane and had to deal with the aftermath of my reckless choices. She did her best to address the reporters who were harassing me." Liddie smiled tightly. "Bitsy—er, Deputy King—might be able to reassure Daisy. Make her feel safe. She's not stern, like Deputy Banks." Liddie stepped closer, trying to catch Jonah's eye as he stared off into the distance, seemingly deep in thought. "We have to see if there's anything about this Dean character we need to worry about."

When Jonah didn't respond, Liddie pressed on. "Bitsy told me to call her if I ever needed anything. She won't mind if this all turns into some misunderstanding."

Jonah's eyes grew hard. "Enough. We need to trust *Gott* and move beyond this. We keep inviting Outsiders onto my farm. Law enforcement leads to news coverage leads to more harassment. We need to put an end to this."

"By ignoring it?" Liddie surprised herself by her sharp outburst.

A muscle ticked in Jonah's jaw.

"I understand your concerns," Liddie said, softening her tone. Of course, Jonah was overwhelmed with his wife's death and having to raise two young children, and now this. "*Yah*, that might happen. But it's a risk we have to take. Even if Daisy is wrong about Dean, I can't ignore the note found tucked in her doll or the fact that Daisy found her way into the neighbor's barn."

"She wanted to see the puppy," Jonah said, barely above a whisper, as if he had spoken aloud a thought he had been trying to rationalize.

"Maybe, but do you think she could have worked the latches? Even so," she said, frustration edging her tone. "It still doesn't explain the note or the smashed flowerpots. What if Daisy ran there to hide? I know you want to protect your family, but we have to alert the sheriff's department in order to do that."

Liddie would never forgive herself if their silence, or their need to follow the tenet of remaining separate, led to Daisy or Andy getting hurt. *"Please."*

Jonah nodded slowly. "We'll call from my business cell phone in the workshop."

SEVEN

A short time later, Deputy Bitsy King pulled up the lane in her personal vehicle. When she climbed out, the off-duty deputy was dressed in civilian clothing and her makeup-free face, her messy bun, and her simple black jacket and jeans with no adornment made Liddie think of the woman's Amish roots. She supposed a person didn't automatically go from wearing plain dresses to high-end fashion, not that she'd know it if she saw it.

"Thanks for coming over, Bitsy," Liddie said. "I didn't realize it was your day off. I would have—"

"I'm glad you called." She smiled and waved her hand, then tucked the tips of her fingers into the front pockets of her jeans. Liddie knew the woman prided herself on bridging the gap between Amish and law enforcement, a mighty wide chasm. "Dispatch knows to reach out to me when one of my Amish friends calls." Bitsy smiled softly and her gaze slid over to Jonah. "Hello. I don't believe we've met."

Liddie made the introductions and then explained what had been going on around the farm over the past few days. She suspected there was no need to go back as far as Maggie Troyer's murder. Any law enforcement officer in Hickory Lane would be up to date on any major crimes in the area. As if reading her mind, the deputy's brow furrowed and she seemed to scan the landscape, including the dilapidated greenhouse that always sent a quiver down Liddie's spine. "I'm terribly sorry about your wife, Mr. Troyer."

Jonah gave a slight nod but didn't say anything.

"You haven't had any trouble since then…until now?" Bitsy probed.

"*Neh*, it's been relatively quiet since the man who murdered my wife was arrested." A muscle worked in his jaw as he relayed the nightmarish events. "The incident with Liddie by the greenhouse came out of nowhere. Then Daisy wandered away and was found trapped in a horse stall. I think someone might have lured her away, but she's not talking about what happened."

"Um…" Liddie hesitated for a moment. "Daisy responded negatively when she saw a van driver here. She claimed he hurt her *mem*."

Bitsy's eyes flashed wide. "Really?"

Jonah shook his head adamantly. "My daughter did not witness her mother's murder."

Bitsy nodded, seemingly taking everything in. "Do you know his name? I can ask around."

"Dean. I don't know his last name, but I recognized him."

The deputy twisted her lips. "Shouldn't be hard to track down a person by that name who hires out to the Amish."

"That's a waste of time," Jonah said.

"Well, tell me about the note you found after Daisy

got trapped in the neighbor's barn." Bitsy wasn't going to let Jonah off the hook. "Do you still have it?"

Liddie glanced over at Jonah, who had taken the piece of paper from her. He shook his head. "I disposed of it."

Bitsy nodded in understanding. "Deputy Banks has been out here." It was more statement than question. "I'll read his reports." Her tone didn't sound hopeful.

"Deputy Banks responded to the call when my wife died and when Liddie was attacked. We didn't trouble him with the more recent events. We... *I* wasn't sure it was worth it. I made sure the property was secure. Whoever had left that note was long gone," Jonah said, as if talking through all the options out loud, perhaps justifying his reasoning for not calling in law enforcement after another suspicious incident on his farm. The Amish might seem naive at times, but they had a strong faith in *Gott* and less in Outsiders.

"Don't ever feel like you're bothering us," Bitsy said. "It's our job to respond to things like this, especially if you think your daughter is in jeopardy."

Jonah's back straightened and his gaze grew steely. "My daughter is safe. I'll make sure of that."

"I'm glad your daughter is fine." Bitsy smiled tightly. "Do you mind if I walk the property?"

Liddie looked to Jonah for consent before answering for him. *"Yah."* But Liddie could tell he was uncomfortable with all of this. It probably stemmed from his Amish roots. The tenet of staying separate was drilled into all of them. Liddie had become more receptive due to gaining a brother-in-law who was in law enforcement and because of Bitsy. The formerly-Amish deputy had used her authority to chase off unwanted photographers and news crews that had invaded tranquil Hickory Lane after they became fascinated with the Amish angle of a major drug bust after her sister's kidnapping.

"I'll show you around," Jonah said. Liddie started to follow as they set off toward the greenhouse when Amity emerged from the path separating their properties. Liddie tried to hide her annoyance. "I'll see what Amity wants."

Jonah tipped his head. The man almost had as few words as his young daughter.

"Guder mariye." Good morning. The teenager hollered her greeting as she quickly closed the gap between them, but her gaze followed Jonah and the officer as they strode toward the greenhouse, leaving Liddie behind to greet their teenage neighbor. "Who's that with Jonah?" Amity asked. The teenager's directness was jarring. It had the desired effect of eliciting an answer, even when Liddie didn't feel like giving one.

"Deputy King."

"Oh? Is this about Daisy getting stuck in the barn?" Amity's thin lips tugged down, and a shadow swept across her face.

Good question. Bitsy should definitely check out the barn, see if she thought Daisy could manipulate the latch. Or maybe his young daughter had let herself in to see the puppies, and the door had swung shut behind her. And whoever left the note could have tucked it in the doll when Daisy dropped it.

How likely was it that Daisy would wander off without her doll? It didn't add up.

Liddie pressed her fingers to her temple, a headache forming behind her eyes. She didn't need to share everything with the neighbor because that's how rumors got started, but Liddie needed to ask a few pointed questions of her own.

"Did you see Daisy wander over to the barn yesterday?"

Amity frowned. *"Neh."* A look of pure innocence with a touch of surprise flashed across her face. "I had no idea Daisy was missing until Mr. Troyer came looking for her." She pressed a hand to her chest. "If I'd had known, I would have brought her right home."

Liddie frowned. "Did you see anyone or anything out of the ordinary yesterday?"

Amity's eyes rounded. "Do you think someone is trying to hurt Daisy? Why?"

Liddie feared she had just fed the gossip mill. "I'm just tired. I don't know what I'm thinking." She did her best to backtrack. "Don't worry. Everything's fine."

Amity made a noise with her lips. "That other deputy was already out here the other night. What's really going on?"

Liddie bit back her annoyance at the girl's inquisitiveness, no small feat considering that same kind of misguided curiosity had made Liddie the subject of constant rumors. "We thought we should report the more recent incidences. Just in case."

Amity pressed a hand to her chest. "Does Jonah really think someone locked Daisy in my family's barn?" She turned her frightened eyes back toward her home. "Maybe I should go warm my *mem*."

"You never told your mother what happened when they got home from delivering the pies?" Liddie crossed her arms and studied the girl.

Amity lowered her gaze and drew an imaginary line

in the grass with her boot. "I might have left the barn door unlatched."

Heat flooded Liddie's face. "You mean, Daisy might have wandered in there because you left the barn door open?" That still didn't explain the threatening note, but Amity didn't know about that.

"I might have been in a hurry to finish my chores so I could lounge around. I love having the house to myself and it never happens." Liddie couldn't imagine the teen ever had a second to herself with all her siblings. With her head still tilted, Amity lifted her gaze to meet Liddie's. "I'm sorry."

Would the little girl have wandered away on her own? Perhaps drawn by the promise of puppies? It didn't ring true no matter how contrite Amity seemed.

"I don't think Daisy would have gone there on her own, especially without her doll." Liddie stared at the ceiling for most of the night worried about this. "Something or someone drew her there." She was more convinced now than ever.

"Maybe she heard the puppies barking?" The question came out on a squeak while Amity fussed with the lapel of her coat. "You don't think that whoever…" The teenager paused, perhaps trying to find the words. "You don't think the person who killed Mrs. Troyer has come back?" The color drained from her face.

"Neh, neh," Liddie tried to reassure her, feeling bad for having frightened her. "Jonah assured me that man died in custody. But just be aware of your surroundings. Okay?"

"*Yah*, I will. Of course," Amity said. Liddie was surprised she didn't see more fear in the young girl's eyes. Perhaps youth and ignorance was a mixed blessing.

"Um, I came over because I wanted to check on Daisy's puppy. Make sure he's doing okay away from his mother."

A flush of hot discomfort pooled under Liddie's arms despite the cool morning air. Why the reluctance? Hadn't Amity been generous in giving Daisy the puppy? The puppy that was drawing her out of her shell. "Come on," Liddie said with forced cheeriness. "They're in the house."

Once inside, they found Daisy sitting cross-legged on the hardwood floor reading a storybook out loud to the puppy, who was sleeping inches away on a few bunched-up blankets. Liddie's heart nearly exploded at the tender gesture. She hadn't realized Daisy could read. Or maybe she was reciting the story from memory. Either way, Andy played nearby ostensibly with his toy cars, but he was definitely tuning in to his favorite story. Ellen could be heard preparing a meal in the kitchen.

"Daisy, look who's here. Amity wanted to say hello to Snowball."

Daisy looked up warily and scooted in front of the makeshift dog bed, blocking their view.

"No one's taking the dog away," Liddie said. "Amity just wants to say hello."

Daisy tipped her head and crossed her arms, immediately reverting into her shell.

Amity held up her hands. "I didn't mean to upset anyone." She smiled brightly and crossed the room. She leaned over Daisy to check on the puppy behind her. "Snowball looks happy here. I'm right next door if you need anything." Amity straightened and joined Liddie at the door. "If Snowball misses his mommy you can bring him over."

When Daisy didn't respond, Liddie said, "Daisy, use your manners." Then to Amity, she said, "I'm sorry. It's been a rough few days."

"I understand," she said, agreeable. "Bye, Daisy." Then, as if it were an afterthought, she said, "Bye, Andy."

Liddie saw Amity out, then turned to Daisy. The hair lifted at the nape of her neck when she caught the child's hard expression.

A mother hen protecting her chick.

Or a wounded child terrified of losing something else she loved?

Jonah walked the deputy to her vehicle where Liddie waited for them. He tracked his teenage neighbor as she slipped through the tall weeds along the path that separated their properties. "What did Amity want?"

"I should go talk to her," Bitsy said before Liddie had a chance to answer. "She was the only one home when Daisy got locked in the barn, right?" She looked to him, then Liddie expectantly.

"No, hold up," Liddie said.

Jonah lifted his eyebrows, waiting.

"Amity said she sometimes forgets to close the barn door when she's in a rush to do her chores." Liddie lifted a shoulder, but she didn't look too convinced. "Perhaps Daisy snuck in and the door swung shut."

"To both the barn and the stall?" Bitsy asked the question they were probably all thinking.

"It doesn't seem likely, but I thought I should tell you," Liddie said. "Amity seems worried about getting in trouble with her parents. Perhaps we can investigate without drawing too much attention?" It seemed Liddie was protective of the young girl, just like she had been protective of his daughter when it came to him. Liddie must have needed an advocate for herself when she lived at home and now wanted to be one for others.

"I'll look around and play it cool," the deputy said. "In the meantime, be vigilant. Lock the doors. Don't venture out alone. Anywhere." Her gaze landed on Liddie. "Keep the children close."

"I will." His nanny's voice cracked. "I won't let them out of my sight."

Bitsy opened the car door, then rested her forearms on the top of the door frame. "Don't blame yourself." Jonah wasn't sure if she was talking to him or Liddie because she split her gaze equally between them. "I will look into this Dean character and next time anything suspicious happens, call me right away."

An unease blanketed Jonah's skin. Why was his farm the target of such evil? He drew in a deep breath. He needed to have more faith that things would turn around. "I believe I scared them away." His fingers twitched at the memory of holding the shotgun as Liddie was being dragged away. "Nothing is going to happen here. I'm done with construction jobs for the season. I won't leave the farm."

He felt the warmth of Liddie's gaze.

"There's no shame in calling us, Mr. Troyer. If you don't want to call 9-1-1, call me directly. We can keep it under the radar."

"I appreciate that, but…" Instead of accepting the deputy's offer, he felt the need to deflect. He so desperately wanted this all to go away.

The deputy lifted her chin a fraction. "You're not alone out here. It's the sheriff's department's job to keep the peace. Despite the rules of the *Ordnung*, I'm telling you there's no shame in calling us." She ducked down and tucked herself behind the steering wheel.

"Guder mariye." Her perfect Pennsylvania Dutch reminded him of her Amish roots.

Bitsy started her vehicle and drove away. Liddie turned to him. "Did you find anything when you walked the property with Bitsy?"

"*Neh*, nothing out of the ordinary." He took a step toward the house and paused. "I'm not sure what we accomplished other than inviting Outsiders onto my land." He hated his mournful tone.

"Jonah..." She called his name and let it hang in the air until he stopped and turned around. "No one is going to look at you differently because of all of this." If Jonah hadn't been watching her, he might have missed the subtle flinch, as if she realized the folly of what she had said as soon as it left her mouth. "Okay, *yah*, people do gawk at us. They like to think that what happened here couldn't possibly happen to them if they follow the rules. But you did follow the rules. Me—" she pressed her hand to her chest "—I made bad choices that led to bad things. But you didn't. You need to stop trying to overcompensate to prove you're worthy."

"Prove I'm worthy." He repeated the words that stung because they hit close to home. When his in-laws had invited their daughter and husband to take over the farm, Maggie's extended family grumbled that Jonah didn't deserve it. Maggie's older sister had more children and a smaller farm. But, for whatever reason, Ellen and Abe Stolzfus had extended the offer to Maggie and Jonah. Secretly, he suspected his in-laws worried that his employment outside of the Amish community would lead to temptation. Working the land was the closest one could get to *Gott.* Yet, Jonah had accepted his in-laws' generous offer of land and home, and none of it worked out the way any of them could have imagined.

Jonah shook away the thoughts crowding his mind and turned to Liddie. Based on the tilt of her head and the question in her eyes, she must have said something when he was distracted. "What?" he said, a little too abruptly, trying to tamp down his self-doubt.

Liddie sighed. "Let's go inside and check on the children."

"Okay," he acquiesced. He turned on his heel and strode quickly to the house, but she kept pace.

"You don't have to give up your construction jobs. I'll make sure the children are safe."

Without slowing down, he climbed the porch steps. "The jobs have dried up with winter coming. I'll take care of my family." He opened the door and allowed her to go ahead of him. Surprise flashed in her eyes.

Or maybe it was wariness.

When he hired a nanny for his children, he had only considered his family's immediate needs. He hadn't anticipated the long winter days ahead of them, both cooped up in the house.

EIGHT

The next day started out much cooler than the previous. Plump bruised clouds hung low on the horizon promising rain, or if the temperatures dropped further, snow. Liddie held her coat together with one hand and hustled from the buggy toward the grocery store entrance, Daisy at her side, her doll tucked close to her face. With the threat of inclement weather, Liddie had convinced Jonah to take Andy and run across the street to get what he needed from the hardware store. And then the four of them could return home. Together.

As the automatic doors whooshed open, Liddie glanced over her shoulder. Jonah stood outside the hardware store, waiting for them to get safely inside. It seemed Jonah took his commitment to not letting them out of his sight seriously.

Daisy hung close as Liddie navigated a small grocery cart through the produce aisles. An elderly Amish woman froze, green apple in hand hovering over the plastic bag, and openly gawked at her. Or maybe at Daisy, the motherless little girl in her charge. She couldn't be certain. Between the two of them, they provided enough fodder for even the busiest flapping jaws in the small town of Hickory Lane. This was the one thing Liddie hadn't missed about coming into town. Tucked away at the Troyer farm, she hadn't been subjected to the blatant stares. She wondered how long she'd be the sister of the Amish girl who was abducted by drug dealers. And would sweet Daisy always be the girl orphaned by a violent murderer?

Instinctively, Liddie reached down and let her fingers brush Daisy's bonnet. It might have been easier for Liddie to jump the fence, like her sister, to escape her past, start fresh, but this little girl tugged at her heartstrings. Liddie had to stay for her. At least until Daisy came out of her shell.

Liddie's thoughts drifted to the girl's father and how protective and loving he had been toward his children as he hurried to get them ready for their trip into town. It was a stark departure from the stoic man who had rushed off to work early every morning. He was revealing a side she hadn't seen since her arrival, and she found herself daydreaming about what it would be like if they were a real family.

Liddie's cheeks flushed at the thought and she lifted her gaze. The woman by the apples continued to shoot critical gazes with an upturned nose in their direction between selecting her produce. Liddie resisted the urge to glare back or make some snappy comment like, "Take a picture, it will last longer," knowing the jab would serve double duty since they were Amish and didn't believe in having their photos taken. Liddie also knew one of the Amish tenets was forgiveness, yet a fair number of her Amish neighbors seemed to be withholding theirs.

Or maybe it was the Bible recommendation, "Judge

not, that ye be not judged," that her critical neighbors chose to ignore.

Liddie shook off her annoyance at the woman's open rudeness and decided to take her own advice and not judge her. Who knew what went on in anyone else's heart? She let out a slow breath and turned to Daisy. "Let's hurry and get what we need so your *dat*'s not waiting on us, okay?"

Daisy nodded and grabbed the side of the cart.

When they were done selecting their items, Liddie asked Daisy if she'd like to choose a treat at checkout.

To Liddie's surprise, Daisy approached the candy display with her cloth doll pressed against her mouth and nose. Liddie had been able to clean the mud off of it in the washbasin. Thankfully, the new puppy had been a nice distraction, allowing time for the doll to dry.

Daisy reached out tentatively and picked up a bag of gummy bears. Liddie bit back a triumphant, "Yes!" and instead smiled encouragingly as the little girl lifted her sad brown eyes to hers. Liddie had feared losing the progress she had made prior to when the girl had gone missing briefly. Liddie still held out hope that the girl would eventually open up to her. But any time Liddie gently broached the subjects of her getting locked in the neighbor's barn or her mother's tragic death, Daisy seemed to retreat into herself. Liddie had to be careful. Hopefully, the child would open up more with time.

Liddie placed her hand on the little girl's bonnet. "I like gummy bears, too."

Daisy nodded her thanks before placing them next to the bread as it moved down the conveyor. Liddie's heart softened. The cashier checked them out and Liddie pushed the cart outside. She had expected Jonah and Andy to be done with their errands already, but she didn't see any sign of them. "Let's put these bags into the buggy and we'll walk over to the hardware store to find your father and brother."

Daisy didn't respond, more focused on poking her little fingers into the candy packet and pulling out a bear. Liddie couldn't help but smile.

Their horse and buggy was hitched to a post next to the sidewalk, one of a few in the grocery store parking lot. Liddie set down the bags and approached the horse from the side and stroked its neck with both hands. "Good girl." She lifted one bag into the back of the buggy. It tipped over, spilling out the apples. It took her a moment to organize the groceries, when she turned and was surprised to see Daisy hanging back. Something about the girl's body language sent a whisper of dread skittering up her spine.

Liddie abandoned the task at hand and rushed across the sidewalk toward Daisy. "Come on, we need to go." Her body had gone rigid, and dark shadows haunted the depths of her eyes. The fear radiating off the child burrowed into Liddie's heart. "Daisy?" Her voice cracked as she moved closer. *Jonah, where are you?* "What's wrong?"

The little girl was lost in a trance. Liddie followed her gaze to the other side of the grocery store entrance. A man sat on the cement windowsill under a sign touting twenty-nine-cent-per-pound bananas. He was drawing deeply on a cigarette and talking agitatedly into a flip phone, his face shielded by the bill of his Buffalo Bills cap. Something about him seemed familiar, but she wasn't interested in drawing his attention.

Liddie got down on eye level with the child. "Daisy, let's get your *dat*, okay?"

Daisy blinked a few times, seeming to finally tune into Liddie.

"Daisy?" Liddie repeated.

The girl dipped her head toward the doll that seemed permanently affixed to the lower half of her face. She lifted her free hand and her gaze narrowed fearfully at the man. *"Neh, neh, neh."* No, no, no.

Alarm raced across Liddie's skin.

Liddie once again glanced over at the man who was now staring at them. *Dean!* She gently lowered Daisy's hand. "Don't point," she whispered. The naked fear on the girl's face sent a flood of adrenaline shooting into Liddie's bloodstream. They had to find Jonah and Andy. Now.

Had Dean followed them here?

"It's okay." Liddie's forced reassurance sounded hollow. She placed her hand at the back of Daisy's bonnet and hustled toward the hardware store. "Let's go find your *dat*."

"Hey!" The man gestured to her with his cigarette pinched between his fingers.

Liddie lifted her chin with a confidence she didn't feel and ignored him.

"Hey, you. I'm talking to you," Dean said more aggressively and he stalked toward them.

Liddie drew up short and shoved Daisy behind her and decided to feign ignorance. "I'm sorry, sir, you'll have to excuse us." Her mind whirled as her heart raced in her throat. Had someone in the sheriff's department talked to him? Shared the child's accusation that he had hurt her mother?

Sweat prickled her hairline as he blocked the sidewalk. Daisy clung to her waist and whimpered.

A slow smile spread across the man's face but didn't reach his hard eyes. "Liddie? Liddie Miller? That *is* you."

She furrowed her brow. *"Yah?"*

"You're Moses's girl." A statement. Not a question. Maybe he didn't know what Daisy had accused him of, after all.

"I'm sorry, I'm in a hurry." She gave him her best pleading look. *Go away!*

"It's Dean. We met at that party," the man pressed on. His voice hit a high note, as if he were offended that she didn't remember him. She got the sense that he was fishing for something.

"That must have been a long time ago." Maybe his appearance here today had been a horrible coincidence.

Dean hitched a shoulder, then pointed at Daisy with his lit cigarette. "What's wrong with her?"

"Nothing." A surge of protectiveness welled up in her chest.

Dean studied Daisy closely, his eyes narrowing. Was he trying to scare her? The cold expression made Liddie shudder. She glanced around. The hardware store was directly across the street. They just had to get across the street. Then she'd find Jonah and they'd be safe.

Liddie forced a cheery smile. "Well, nice to see you, Dean." God would forgive her a little white lie. "I have to meet someone now."

"Not sure why you're in such a hurry. I was only trying to say hello," he called after her. "I heard you're a nanny now. Over at the Troyers' place on Windy Road."

"I really have to go." Liddie waved a hand without turning around. She checked both ways and rushed across the street with Daisy still clinging to her side. When they reached the sidewalk, Liddie bent down to look Daisy in the eye. "Are you okay?"

Daisy's wide-eyed gaze drifted across the street. Dean stared at them through a cloud of cigarette smoke.

"Come on," Liddie said, taking the girl's cold hand, and opening the door to the hardware store. "Let's get your *dat*."

Jonah looked up when Liddie and his daughter bustled into the hardware store. Something about the expression on Liddie's face and the frightened way Daisy hung close to her sent fear pressing into his heart. He set his package of sandpaper and bottle of wood preservative down on the counter. "I'll be right back," he said to the clerk. "Come on, Andy." He gently tapped his son's shoulder and they rushed over to Liddie and Daisy. "Is something wrong?" Jonah glanced toward the street, but flyers in the window blocked his view.

"Dean," Liddie said in a hushed whisper, "the driver of that van at the house the other day, was in the parking lot of the grocery store." Her protective hand shielded Daisy's ears.

Jonah gritted his teeth. "I should have never left you two alone." He thought he could run over to the hardware store and be back to the grocery store before they finished. When would he ever learn? Rage clouded his thoughts. "Did he do something?"

"Neh." Liddie's brow twitched, as if she was trying to make sense of it herself. "It seemed like he wanted to let us know he was there." She hesitated a beat. "And that he knows I'm your nanny." Her lower lip quivered

for the briefest of moments before her lips flattened into a straight line as she fought her emotions.

"Do you think he followed us?" Jonah kept his voice down, too, so as not to frighten the children. "Stay right here," he added, without waiting for an answer and he stepped outside. The clouds had grown darker and a brisk wind tugged at his felt hat. His eyes scanned the street and the grocery store parking lot. A red van inched out from behind a pickup truck deep in the parking lot. It drove slowly to the exit, then turned onto Main Street in front of him. The van stopped and the window lowered. The driver lifted his lit cigarette to his lips, inhaled deeply, then exhaled sharply, the cloud of smoke billowing out of the open window. Jonah took a step toward him, to confront him.

Did this man have something to do with his wife's death? Had he been with the accused murderer Oliver Applegate? But why taunt his family? Was he that sick?

Anger and rage clawed at his throat as Jonah stormed into the street.

Dean's eyes seemed to flash momentarily in surprise. Then the *Englischer* lifted his cigarette hand and gave Jonah a sly smile, then stepped on the gas. The tires spun out, leaving skid marks in the street and a burnt rubber smell clogging the air.

"Leave us alone," Jonah hollered to the back of the van as it careened at a high rate of speed around the corner. "Leave us alone!"

He spun on his heel and returned to the hardware store where Liddie held each of his children's hands. His entire body vibrated from the confrontation.

"What happened?" Liddie asked, still keeping her voice low.

Jonah glanced down at Daisy, who was studying the floor from behind her doll, and then to Andy, who was watching him closely. “Everything is okay. Nothing to worry about,” he said for his son’s benefit. “Can you guys wait right here while I pay the clerk?” He had to get them home.

Liddie nodded tentatively, still looking every bit as frightened as she had when she and Daisy burst into the hardware store. He smiled at her, trying to telegraph his reassurance. “Wait right here,” he repeated. “Don’t go outside without me.”

“Why, *Dat*?” Andy asked. “Is there a bad man out there?”

Jonah hadn’t anticipated that question so he hesitated a fraction, then said, “*Neh*, son. There’s no bad man out there. No need to worry.” At that, Daisy hitched her shoulders a fraction closer to Liddie, obviously the less trusting of his children. “It’s cold out. Wait till I pay for my things and then we’ll head out together.”

“Can I help you sand the wood to make it smooth?” Andy asked, the way kids tended to jump from topic to topic. Before Liddie had arrived, Jonah had been explaining some of the tools of his trade to his young son.

“*Yah*, son, we can.” Jonah gave a quick nod of his head, then rushed over to the counter and pulled out a few bills to pay for the supplies. His eye was drawn to the shotguns lined up in a locked case along the back wall. He thought about his own weapon that was once his father-in-law’s. Jonah wasn’t a hunter, so until the night he had grabbed it to protect Liddie, he had no use for it.

Apparently following his gaze, the clerk asked, “Can I pull something down for you to look at?”

Jonah glanced back at his little family. His family? Was he starting to consider Liddie as part of his family? The way she was crouched down in front of his children and engaging them warmed his heart. If he had done anything right in recent months, it had been hiring warm and endearing Liddie Miller. His daughter had even pulled the doll away from her face to talk to her.

Jonah shifted his attention back to the clerk. "I have a shotgun, but not much ammunition."

"What kind do you need?" The clerk's eyes sparked to life in a way they hadn't when he was selling boring woodworking supplies.

Jonah shared what he knew about the shotgun. The clerk braced his hands on the edge of the counter and leaned forward, as if settling in to tell him a story. "I have one of those myself. Now, I have a few different kinds of bullets. What are you hunting?"

A ticking sounded in Jonah's temple as he considered the question. *Human beings?* The thought made him shudder.

"Ah, deer hunting?" The statement came out more like a question.

"Well, I have a couple kinds for that." The clerk levered off the counter and crouched down, apparently reading box labels stashed below. He pulled out a small box and set it on the smooth surface, its contents shifting with a clinking noise. "I recommend this type. Take a deer out right quick. As long as you're a good shot," the salesman added with a slanted smile. "If you're a bad shot it doesn't make no difference what kind of bullet you got."

"True," Jonah muttered, hating the idea of shooting anything. "I'll take it."

He had to be ready.

To protect his family.

NINE

Liddie had trouble sleeping that night after their run-in with Dean in the parking lot at the grocery store. *What if Jonah hadn't been nearby? What if she had been unable to keep Daisy safe?*

What if...? What if...? What if...?

The barrage of worries pinging in her head kept her awake all night. As the sleepless hours stretched on, she grew increasingly frustrated that no one seemed to want to investigate Dean as a possible suspect in Maggie Troyer's death.

Oliver Applegate's fingerprints were all over the murder weapon, so why should they bother with Dean? That seemed to be the consensus. That, and the belief that Daisy was a confused and traumatized little girl.

When the first hint of dawn softened the dark shadows of her room, Liddie stopped pretending she was going to get any sleep. She flung the quilt back and got out of bed and ready for the day. It was Sunday, but the Amish only held services every other week. She was relieved that today was an "off Sunday" and she wouldn't have to face the community and their curious stares. However, her relief was short-lived when

Ellen announced they were going to visit her daughter in nearby Apple Creek. Not in the mood to be scrutinized by Jonah's dead wife's family, Liddie asked to be dropped off at home. She hadn't been there since she left for this job, and she couldn't avoid them forever. Besides, she hoped to shut down any rumors they might have heard about her.

Would she ever get out of the spotlight?

Thankfully, when Jonah turned the buggy up the lane of her childhood home, she spotted her grandfather sitting in the rocker on the stoop of his *dawdy haus.* He lifted his pipe in greeting. His welcoming smile dispelled any doubts that she had about stopping by for a visit. She had really missed him.

Liddie hopped out of the buggy and looked up at Jonah and a warm flush heated her cheeks when she found him watching her. *"Denki,"* she said shyly as she stepped away from the buggy.

Wide-eyed, Andy jumped to his feet and peeked out from behind a wall that shielded the back seat from view. "Are you coming back, Miss Liddie?"

His earnest question caught her off guard. Her gaze automatically went to Jonah's. More than once she had offered to leave for good and more than once, he had insisted she stay. But right now, his stoic expression made her wonder if he was just being polite. What was going on behind those serious brown eyes? Maybe yesterday's excitement had been the last straw. Maybe that's why he hadn't insisted she come with them to his former in-laws'. Her heart thudded in her ears and she forced a bright smile for the benefit of the children. "Of course, I'll be back in the morning."

"*Dat* said we're sleeping in our own beds tonight."

Liddie could imagine Jonah reassuring his children that they wouldn't be staying overnight at his in-laws, yet she wondered how Ellen felt about that.

Making a point not to look at Jonah, Liddie reached into the back of the buggy and patted Snowball. Daisy had refused to go anywhere without her new puppy. Her doll was squished into the seat between her and the wall. "I'll see you both tomorrow."

"Will you be home in time for breakfast?" Andy asked, sliding back into his seat.

Liddie smiled again. If she could only bottle this boy's forthrightness. "As soon as my brother is done with his morning chores, he'll bring me right—" She had been about to say the word *home*, but stopped herself short. "He'll bring me back," she finally settled on saying.

Liddie grabbed her small cloth bag with some overnight essentials and watched Jonah turn the buggy around and leave.

"The prodigal granddaughter has returned," her grandfather said.

"Only for the night." She scanned the familiar landmarks and surprisingly tears pricked the back of her eyes.

"I heard there was some excitement at the Troyer farm."

Liddie's shoulders sagged. "Nice to know some things never change." The Amish tongues wagged at a speed that could rival the internet.

"Wie bischt du heit?" How are you today?

"Ich bin gut." I've been good.

Her grandfather bit the mouthpiece of his pipe and tilted his head, as if to say, "Are you sure?"

"*Yah*, I just wanted to see everyone. Jonah and his children are visiting relatives and I feared I'd be in the way." She clasped her bag in front of her and her eyes went to her childhood home. "I suppose I shouldn't put off the inevitable."

"I suppose you shouldn't." Her grandfather puffed on his pipe. "Make sure you spend some time with me before you go."

"Of course." Her grandfather had been a calming force in their family. First with her sister Bridget and her decision to leave the Amish and now with her. Despite his conservative roots, he seemed to be able to find love and acceptance more readily than her own parents. She suspected it was because he had his own more circuitous path to Amish baptism than most, making him more understanding of her struggle.

Liddie let out a long breath and climbed the steps of her childhood home. She lifted her hand to knock, not really sure if she should. She never had to knock before. But something compelled her to.

Her mother answered the door, her curious gaze morphing into pure joy. Her hands flew to her face. "You're home!"

"Hello, *Mem*." Emotion clogged her throat. She had missed seeing her mother dearly. The tiny scar on her cheek from where a branch had caught her when she was a little girl. The way her nose scrunched up when she smiled. The patches of gray hair that seemed to frizz just a bit more than the brown hair around the edges of her bonnet after standing over the stove.

Liddie had missed *everything* about her mother.

"Willkumm. Willkumm." Welcome. Her mother stepped back to allow Liddie entrance. "Did you eat

breakfast? Your father and brothers are in the barn doing their morning chores. They'll be so happy to see you."

Liddie smiled tightly, not wanting to burst her mother's bubble. Her father would not be happy to see her. She set her things down on a bench inside the door. "Can I help with breakfast?"

"Yah." Her mother breezed into the kitchen and the two of them worked on preparing scrapple and a huge bowl of scrambled eggs.

As Liddie stood side-by-side with her mother, she realized how much she had missed being part of a family. The Troyer children, especially Andy, had developed a certain fondness for her, but their grandmother had kept her at arm's length, refusing to allow her to help in the kitchen. Daisy had wanted so desperately to connect, but couldn't get past her grief. And Jonah seemed to be guided by a sense of guilt and reluctance to move past the tragic loss of his wife.

"How are the children?" her mother asked, drying her hands on her apron.

"Andy is very precocious. Reminds me of Caleb and Elijah when they were younger."

"Your brothers were a handful," her mother said wistfully. "How is the girl?"

"Daisy's very quiet."

Her mother made a noise with her lips. "I can't imagine how hard it was to lose her mother." Her own mother's eyes grew red. "I've missed you."

"Me, too, *Mem*."

"I wish you could stay longer than one night." Her gaze suddenly drifted to beyond Liddie's shoulder and her lips twitched. Butterflies flitted in Liddie's stomach as she turned around. Her father stood in the mudroom, still in his coat and boots.

"Guder mariye, Dat." Good morning.

"Lydia." Her father used her formal name, causing her to brace for whatever would come next. "I didn't know you were coming. Did you lose your job?" The accusation in his tone stabbed her heart, and her disappointment was mirrored in her mother's pained expression.

"*Nah*, I did not lose my job," she said evenly.

"Amos, Liddie came for a visit." That was her mother's nonconfrontational way of saying, "Please, let it go."

"I heard there was trouble on the Troyer farm?" her father pressed on.

Liddie felt her face growing hot. "*Yah*, there has been."

A muscle started to tick in her father's jaw, and instead of trying to defend herself—from what, she wasn't sure—she let the silence stretch between them. Finally, he said, "I hope you had nothing to do with it."

Before Liddie had a chance to answer, her youngest brother, Caleb, looking so grown up at thirteen, wandered into the house followed by a more subdued Elijah, who at seventeen was probably starting to think about finding a nice Amish girl to settle down with.

"Hey, Liddie," Caleb said, while sliding into his usual seat at the kitchen table. She loved how he treated her appearance like any other morning.

"Sight for sore eyes," Elijah said, his eyes twinkling. At least her brothers seemed happy to see her.

"Wash up, boys. Then, let's all sit and eat. Like old times."

Liddie took her place at her usual seat to the left of Elijah. Her father sat at the head of the table. They bowed their heads and said a silent prayer of thanks. Then her father picked up his fork and began to eat, his anger radiating off of him.

Liddie knew exactly what it meant.

How dare she bring shame once again to their family.

Liddie picked up her fork. Her mother was right. Just like old times.

"It's a little chilly out here." Ruthann, Maggie's older sister, slipped outside to join Jonah where he had gone to escape Maggie's extended family. Jonah's visits to Apple Creek since Maggie's death had grown few and far between.

"Just needed a moment." Jonah took off his hat and ran a hand over his head, then stuffed it back on. He leaned back in the rocker.

"We miss the kids," Ruthann said, wrapping her arms tighter around her middle and rolling up on the balls of her feet. "How are they?"

Jonah kept his gaze on the land in front of him. Ruthann and her husband had ten children and a bustling farm, the model Amish family. He couldn't help but feel envious, an emotion he was ashamed of.

"Jonah?" Ruthann leaned forward. "You okay?"

He rocked back and forth slowly, considering. "Just thinking of how things should have been different."

"*Gott* had a plan."

He made a noncommittal sound, then decided to answer her original question. "Andy is great. Loves the nanny. Daisy is still quiet, but seems to be doing better now that Liddie is here. I'm sure you heard about the puppy." He shifted to look at her. "Can you believe we let him sleep in the house?"

"Poor Daisy. She reminds me so much of my sister. It must be too quiet around that big farm."

Jonah couldn't help but bristle. When Ruthann and Maggie's parents had offered their farm to their youngest daughter, there was some resentment.

"Daisy needs her family," Ruthann said, tucking her coat under her and lowering herself onto the rocker. She let out a tired sigh. Across the field, a few of the boys kicked a ball around while their sisters spun in circles, creating fans with their skirts.

Jonah cut his sister-in-law a sideways glance, but she didn't seem to notice. "She has a family," he said, not bothering to soften his tone.

Ruthann wrapped her fingers around the ends of the armrests. "Maggie's family." She waited a beat, then added, "Imagine how she'd thrive with all her cousins around. She wouldn't have time to sulk."

Jonah sucked in a breath, tamping down his anger. His sweet daughter had every right to sulk, as his sister-in-law referred to his daughter's grief. "Daisy lost her mother."

"All the more reason. I'd be happy to take in Daisy and Andy. Then you can go off and do your thing." Ruthann's disdain for his construction work was palpable. It always had been. That had been the crux of the argument when Ellen and Abe had passed on the family farm to Maggie and Jonah and not Ruthann and her family. Land among the Amish was at a premium. Ruthann always complained their house in Apple Creek was too small for their large family. Why did Maggie need such a large plot of land when her husband didn't even farm?

"I have a nanny to watch the children," Jonah said, suddenly wondering what Liddie was up to at this very moment.

"I've heard about this nanny." The derision in Ruthann's tone was unmistakable. "Mother has told me all about her. She's not a good influence on the children. You're not thinking clearly." Ruthann reminded Jonah of Ellen. Made sense since they were mother and daughter. "Please, let my mother and the children stay here with us. We'll make plans to sell this property and move to Hickory Lane as soon as possible." Her brow furrowed. "It might take until spring to sell this place, but we should put the plan in motion as soon as possible."

Jonah narrowed his gaze. "Where am I supposed to live? Are you suggesting I give up my children? My home?"

Ruthann folded her hands in her lap and pushed against the wood planks with the heel of her boot, rocking slowly back and forth. "You have a lot to figure out, Jonah." Her calm tone made him uneasy. She had obviously been considering this for awhile. Maggie's older sister had coveted his home long before his life had been upended.

Hot blood roared through his veins, making it hard to keep his temper in check and his thoughts straight. "Ruthann, I'm not abandoning my children or my home. Besides, that's two more mouths to feed. You already have your hands full."

"We always have room for more." Ruthann lowered her voice. "You never wanted that big old farm. I hear you haven't planted crops since before Father died." She placed her palms together and pressed the tips of her fingers to her lips. "You can work your construction jobs without the hassle and responsibility of the farm."

"Where am I supposed to live? I moved there to help your parents." Jonah was trying to process her outrageous suggestion.

"Your intentions were good when you moved to Hickory Lane to help my parents. I know that." Her condescending tone ripped right through him. "Now it's time to let me and my husband take care of things." Ruthann tilted her head, as if she were now just sorting this all out when, in fact, Jonah had obviously been invited here for this exact conversation. "Maybe you can move in with your brother? Didn't he move to Buffalo?" His brother had moved to Buffalo and his brother was also former Amish. That was not an option.

Jonah tapped the porch railing with his fist. "*Neh*, you are not taking my children. You are not moving into my home." He stomped past her and went into the house. Andy was playing with Matchbox cars in the corner with two of his cousins who were of similar age. Daisy was standing on a step stool next to an older cousin helping to prepare dinner. He grabbed the back of a chair to steady himself. The walls of the small home crowded in on him. Was he being selfish? Would his children be better off growing up with their cousins?

Jonah stuffed down his anger and joined the men who were setting up extra chairs and tables for dinner. He might have been offended by Ruthann's offer, but he wasn't going to cut short their visit because of it. With winter coming soon, it might be awhile before they came back again—if ever.

His gaze drifted to Ellen, who sat reading a story to one of her youngest grandchildren.

Indecision tightened in his chest. Did he owe Maggie's family this? What about his children? Would they be better off?

What about Liddie? His pretty nanny's name whispered through his brain.

Gott, *help me do what's right for my family.*

TEN

As the sun set over her childhood farm, Liddie grabbed her coat and a quilt and went out and sat on the back porch. Her father was inside reading the Bible and her mother was knitting. After trying to make small talk in the sitting room thick with the tension of a family who couldn't see eye-to-eye, she had to get some fresh air. Coming home had been a very, very bad idea. Her father's anger rolled off him in waves. She supposed he was doing his best to shun her. To use one of the best-known Amish tools to pressure his wayward daughter to fall in line. Didn't he realize his tactics might have the opposite effect? Now, if she felt compelled to leave the Troyers' farm to protect the children, she'd have no place to go. He'd force her hand. The end result could be her moving to Virginia to live with her sister until she figured out her next step.

Was that what he really wanted?

Liddie adjusted the quilt over her legs in the chilly night air. She drew in a deep breath and held the collar of her coat closed. She loved the fresh smell of country air as the land settled in for the long winter ahead. The sweet smell of cornstalks ready to be ground for feed mixed with the manure-rich soil. She closed her eyes and Jonah's handsome face came to mind. She wondered if he'd ever farm the land, or if he'd continue to travel to Buffalo for construction jobs once the weather turned to spring again. What kind of family life would that be? Left alone on the farm for long days.

The door creaked and her eyes flew open. Despite the darkness, her face flushed at her thoughts. As if she and Jonah and the kids would someday be a family. She shifted toward the door. Her brother had his shoulders hunched and was making an effort to be stealthy in closing the door.

"Hey, Elijah," she whispered from the shadows, a slight lilt to her voice as she stifled a giggle.

He startled. "Oh, I didn't see you there."

"Sneaking out?" Liddie laughed.

"Well, not exactly. They know I'm going to meet up with friends, but I wanted to get out before *Dat* decided he wants me to muck out the stalls."

"Didn't you do that earlier today?"

"*Yah*, but you know Father. The horses never stop doing their business, and he might just ask me to do it again so I can't meet my friends."

"Sounds like something *Dat* would do."

Elijah slipped into the rocker next to hers and leaned in conspiratorially. "We all miss you, you know."

Liddie nodded, not trusting her voice.

"How is it at the Troyers'? What's it like?" he asked.

"The kids are *gut*."

In the dark she could feel Elijah smiling at her, the way he did when he was a kid with a secret to tell.

"What?"

"I heard *Mem* and *Dat* talking. They're hoping you get married to Jonah."

A strangled laugh escaped her lips and she sputtered, unable to formulate a response. Was that why they had sent her there to work? To marry her off?

"I'm the nanny," she finally said. "I watch his children. That's all."

Elijah planted his hands on the arms of the chair and stood. "Whatever you say."

She was about to protest, but she knew her brother would see it as an opportunity to ramp up his teasing. She changed the subject instead. "Where exactly are you going?"

The moonlight caught Elijah's teeth in a half smile. "Bonfire in the woods."

"I remember those bonfires." She playfully wagged her finger at him. "Be safe."

"Always." Elijah bounced down the steps of the porch and she called after him.

"Any chance Moses Lapp and his friends still hang out at those bonfires?"

"*Yah*, Moses is there a lot." He walked toward her, his face unreadable in the shadows. "What do you want with him? He doesn't have the greatest reputation." Moses had courted Bridget and when that didn't work out, he started to come around to see Liddie, until he finally got the hint that neither Miller sister was interested in him.

"Trust me, I have no interest in Moses beyond information." Liddie didn't want to explain further. The less her brother knew, the better. She pushed to her feet and dropped the quilt over the back of the rocker. "Want some company?"

Liddie felt, rather than saw her little brother roll his eyes. "Come on. We'll take Brownie. She could use the exercise." He turned and rushed toward the barn and Liddie followed, excited to take her favorite horse out for a bit—and to maybe get some dirt on Dean once and for all.

Liddie and Elijah fell into an easy conversation as they rode the horse and buggy to the bonfire. She had really missed her brother. When he turned onto Windy Road she found herself keeping an eye out for the Troyer farm. As they passed, she noticed a single light glowing from the sitting room, and she couldn't help but wonder whether it was Jonah or Ellen still up at this hour. A strange sense of homesickness constricted her heart.

Elijah nudged her elbow. "Just a job, huh?"

"Ha-ha," she said, pulling her coat closer around her neck. She playfully pointed to the dark country road in front of them. "Pay attention."

A short time later, Elijah turned the buggy in to a field. Several other horse and buggies—and a few cars—were lined up in no apparent order. Not all of the cars belonged to *Englischers.* Driving a car was one of those quietly tolerated passages of *Rumspringa* parents prayed their children—mostly sons—outgrew. Liddie couldn't help but wonder what her brother's plans were considering one sister had already jumped the fence and the other seemed to have one foot over it.

Liddie hopped down from the buggy, the long grass crunching under her feet. One of the weeds tickled her bare leg under her dress. When she was Elijah's age, she often snuck out in jeans and a sweatshirt, but now it felt less like sneaking if she, at least, had on plain clothing. Besides, she would have had to dig out her old *Englisch* clothes and that felt like too much premeditation. She feared if their father caught her, she'd lose all hope of reconciling.

The pair followed the loud voices and the laughing and the scent of burning wood along a small path. She cut a sideways glance to her brother who grabbed a beer and peeled back the aluminum tab and offered her one. She waved it away.

"Suit yourself," Elijah said, and slipped through the crowd to find a seat on a log next to a girl. *Hmmm?* Liddie would have to ask him about her later. Their age difference meant that they had never socialized together prior to now. He was seven years younger. Yet, it really hadn't been that long ago that gatherings like these were the highlight of her week. She had loved the socialization, the freedom, the attention from boys. Sure, she had tried a beer or two, before deciding it wasn't for her. She had never been into drugs and she hoped her brother knew enough to avoid them, too.

The temperature was fairly mild for November, but she felt compelled to wrap her coat tightly around her. She took a seat on an empty log and tried to blend in, but felt like she stuck out like a sore thumb. She scanned the faces lit by flickering orange flames. Her heart rate spiked when her gaze landed on Moses Lapp, the man she was looking for. He was staring at her and gave her a subtle nod before throwing his head back to empty his beer. He pitched the can into the dark and stood.

Pulse ticking wildly in her ears, she watched as he found his way over to her and joined her on the log, closer than was warranted. If she didn't need to talk to him, she would have gotten up to leave.

Moses leaned in, the stale smell of beer on his breath. "Jonah Troyer let you out of his sight?"

"Night off." Liddie forced a casual tone. How did he know she worked for Jonah Troyer? Her face grew hot despite the cool November evening. Moses had always stirred up a bit of trouble, first by courting her sister and then turning his attention toward her. However, Liddie quickly grew disinterested for two reasons: her loyalty to her sister and his loyalty to questionable friends.

"Well, then…" Moses leaned away. Light from the bonfire flickered in his penetrating gaze. "How's Bridget?"

"*Gut*, she's married and living near Washington, DC."

"To that law enforcement guy?"

"*Yah*, DEA agent. She's finishing up her advanced degree. She's going to be a nurse practitioner."

Moses adjusted his hat farther back on his thick head of hair. He looked up at the starry sky. A thin gossamer of clouds drifted across the moon. "I never pegged her as one to stay."

Liddie couldn't help but wonder what he pegged *her* for, then wondered why she cared. Perhaps because she herself was so lost.

"What brought you out here? Tired of playing nanny?"

Liddie glanced around to make sure no one was listening. They all seemed more interested in their little cliques and flirting with one another. "I needed to ask you something."

Moses cupped one hand around his ear and slanted her a smug expression as if to say, "I'm all ears."

Liddie cleared her throat, stalling for a fraction longer and feeling like she was about to open a Pandora's box. "Are you still friends with Dean? I can't remember his last name."

"I only know one Dean. Dean Johnson."

"*Yah*, that's him. Dean Johnson."

Moses jerked his head back and laughed. "You looking to be set up? Jump the fence like your sister?" Sarcasm dripped from his words, making icy dread pool in her stomach.

Liddie ignored his comment. "Someone seems to think he was hanging around the Troyers' farm around the time Mrs. Troyer was murdered."

Moses ran the flat of his hand across his smooth-shaven jaw. "I thought they caught the guy who did that."

"They did." Hot blood chugged through her veins like molasses, forcing her to tug on her collar. "What if the guy they arrested wasn't alone?"

Moses drew his eyebrows down, then leaned closer. "Why are you asking about Dean specifically?"

"I saw him driving a van the other day. Came to the farm to pick up a furniture order from Jonah." She purposely left off the part about Daisy being afraid of him. She refused to put the child in jeopardy.

"Seems like a legit way to make some cash."

"Is he still involved in other ways to make money? Maybe not so legit." Liddie had personally seen him try to sell weed to a group of Amish boys while they were all hanging out around a bonfire a few years ago.

Moses's expression grew pinched. "You need to stop asking questions."

"Tell me what you know and I will." She clamped her jaw to stop it from shaking.

"Come with me." Moses tugged her up from her seat on the log and led her away from the bonfire into the dark.

Unease slowed her pace. She pulled her arm away and spun around to face him. "Stop. I'm not going any farther with you."

"*You* need to stop. I thought you learned your lesson after what happened to your sister."

"Bridget? What does this have to do with her?"

"Well, I'd think you'd be tired of courting trouble."

Liddie persisted. "You need to tell me what you've heard about Dean."

A muscle ticked in his jaw. "You're not going to let this go?"

Liddie stood her ground as a swell of nausea rolled over her.

"Okay, Dean is still into drugs." Moses bounced on the balls of his feet as if this whole conversation was making him jittery. "Not me, though. I heard he was growing marijuana on unused land." He frowned. "Any chance Jonah Troyer doesn't know what's going on under his nose?"

Tall weeds grew where corn or other crops had once grown. "Jonah Troyer doesn't farm the land."

"It's possible then." Moses rubbed the back of his neck. "Leave it alone. I'd hate for something to happen to you."

The intense way Moses stared at her made goose bumps race across her skin.

"Don't tell anyone I was asking." Liddie held up her chin, feigning confidence as an unsettling feeling weighed on her chest. Her eyes darted around the black trees surrounding them and she suddenly had the unmistakable feeling that someone was watching them. "Please, keep this quiet."

ELEVEN

Liddie couldn't wait to leave the bonfire. Was Dean—or one of his friends—using Jonah's land to grow marijuana?

Liddie dipped her head and navigated around a group of young men with camouflage-patterned coats and matching baseball caps as they smoked cigars and laughed a few feet away from the crackling bonfire. A part of her wondered if they had wandered over from a nearby hunting cabin. Dismissing the thought, she sought out Elijah and finally found him with a group of friends of mostly familiar Amish faces, laughing and seemingly carefree. When he saw her, he stood and came over. "What's wrong?"

"I want to leave." She tried to keep her voice even.

"Already? We haven't been here that long." Liddie's mind flashed back to all the times her little brother had talked her into playing *one more* board game with her or somehow finagled her to do his chores for him. He was a very charismatic and persuasive kid, but she wasn't having any of it. Not tonight. The puzzle pieces were starting to snap together and she wanted to get back to the Troyer farm. Tell Jonah what she had learned.

"We'll go in like an hour, maybe," Elijah said, his words a bit slurred from alcohol. Liddie couldn't wait that long. She'd crawl out of her skin.

"What if I took the horse and buggy? I want to go back to the Troyers'."

"Now? I thought you were staying at the house overnight?" The disappointment in his tone was like an arrow to the heart. She really did miss her family.

"I need to get back." She didn't want to explain. "*Dat* won't miss Brownie for a day or two." Her family had more than one horse and Brownie had been mostly hers to use when she was still living at home. She had been the one to name her when she was a teenager. "You could swing by the Troyers' in a day or two. Bring my bag and then see that Brownie gets home?" Her tone was hopeful. Anything she had in that bag she could make do without for a few days. "Can you catch a ride home with someone else tonight?"

The kid sitting next to him nodded. He didn't look familiar to Liddie. She wasn't sure if he was Amish or *Englisch.* She was about to agree when she asked, "Have you been drinking, too?"

"No, ma'am. I have a car and I never drink when I'm driving." She studied him for a minute, his gaze sincere in the firelight.

Elijah patted his friend's arm in a jovial manner. "Lenny's a good kid. He'll get me home safe and sound." Then her brother seemed to sober a bit. "Are you sure you don't mind going alone?"

Liddie shook her head. "I'm going directly to the Troyers'. It's not far. We passed it on the way here."

Elijah waved his hand. "Sure, sure. You're going back

to your job." He enunciated the last word like a person who might regret his drink choices in the morning.

"Let *Mem* and *Dat* know where I am."

"Yah." Another friend handed Elijah a beer.

"Don't drink too much, okay?" Liddie hesitated for a fraction, then said, "I'll see you soon." She spun on her heel and hustled through the dark path, suddenly questioning if her decision to travel alone was a good one. The Troyer farm wasn't far. She'd be home in no time, she reassured herself.

"Hey, girl," Liddie said as she patted Brownie, an old friend. "Ready to go?" The horse lifted its head and neighed as Liddie untied her from a nearby tree.

Liddie hopped up onto the buggy bench and made a clicking noise with her tongue and the horse lurched forward, easing out of the field, then up onto the dark country road.

Liddie held the reins with one hand and the coat of her collar tight with the other against a brisk wind. The late evening had grown downright chilly, especially now that she was away from the roaring flames of the bonfire. The Troyer farm was a short buggy ride away. Yet, the lonely country road stretched ominously ahead of her. Tree branches created a shadowy tunnel. The residents of the dark farmhouses were sleeping. A familiar dread crept up her spine.

"Come on, girl." Liddie gently flicked the reins, and her voice seemed to echo in the quiet night. The headlights from a vehicle bore down on her from behind and she edged the buggy toward the side of the road, careful to avoid the ditch. The car passed with a whoosh, and the red taillights disappeared in the black of night, leaving her and Brownie alone with the steady clip-clop-clip of hooves on the asphalt.

A sharp noise—like a gunshot—rang out and sent Liddie's heart racing. She clung tightly to the reins as Brownie reared up and neighed. The buggy bobbled on the edge of a black ditch. Then the buggy suddenly pitched precariously and a scream ripped from her throat. She dropped the reins and clawed at the bench until the horse bucked, tossing her into a cold wet puddle, knocking the wind out of her.

Gasping for breath, Liddie rolled up onto all fours and coughed and sputtered. The freezing water jolted her. Gingerly, she put one foot, then the other under her. She dipped forward and braced herself against the mushy sides of the ditch. Righting herself, she swiped the gritty dirt from her hand onto her coat. Her ankle ached, but she didn't think anything was broken. Above her head the hazy moon glowed and the knobby branches swayed and clacked in the wind.

She breathed in deeply, grateful to fill her lungs with the cool night air.

How am I going to get out of here?

The sound of tires on gravel made her breath hitch. She was unsure if this was a good or bad development. She glanced around, pulling at the fabric of her heavy, wet dress. Her teeth chattered. There was nowhere to go.

"Hel-lo," a male voice called. Footsteps sounded closer. "Is someone there?" He obviously saw the horse and buggy on the side of the road. He was a good Samaritan, stopping to help. Right?

Her jaw ached from the trembling. Was this person harmless? Liddie didn't know if she should remain quiet or acknowledge her presence. Was he truly here to help?

Before she had a chance to make a decision, a beam of light swung across her face. She squeezed her eyes shut, then held up her hand to block the blinding light.

"You okay?" he asked. "Here." He turned off the flashlight. She blinked and the outline on a man in a ball cap came into fuzzy focus. He planted his feet partially down the side of the ditch and extended his hand. "Come on."

Liddie accepted his hand and he pulled her up. She couldn't make out his face under the bill of his hat, but something about him seemed familiar. "Thank you," she said, feeling the weight of her wet dress pulling her down. She rushed over to Brownie and patted her neck. "You okay, girl?" The horse jostled forward and back. Liddie continued to stroke the animal. "It's okay, it's okay."

Even as she reassured the horse, Liddie's legs felt like jelly. The thought of climbing up onto the buggy bench and riding along the darkened road was unappealing. Yet, here she was exposed, alone on a dark road with a stranger. "Thank you for your help." She hurried to the bench and planted her hands on the edge of the buggy and was about to climb in. Her trembling arms didn't want to do their job.

"Come on, I'll drive you home." He tapped the hood of his truck. "My son can take your horse and buggy home."

The passenger door clicked open and a young man climbed out dressed in a camouflage jacket and ball cap. A fresh blanket of goosebumps raced across her flesh. Had he been one of the guys hanging around the bonfire?

The man standing on the road apparently saw her

apprehension and laughed. “I didn’t realize you didn’t recognize me. It’s Deputy Eddie Banks.” He lifted his baseball cap a fraction, then settled it back down on his balding head. He smiled and a whiff of stale beer reached her nose.

Her body sagged in relief. “*Neh*, I hadn’t realized it was you. I’ve only seen you in uniform. And…” she laughed as a wave of embarrassment coursed through her “…I’m a little out of sorts.”

“Completely understandable. Just coming home from picking up my son at one of those parties.” He leaned in conspiratorially. “You remember those days.”

“Funny thing, I had been at the same bonfire with my brother.” Her lips, her face, her entire body felt numb. She figured there was no use in lying. His son was bound to recognize her.

The deputy made a noise she couldn’t quite interpret.

Liddie crossed her arms tightly over her middle. “Did either of you hear a gunshot?”

“No, is that what happened here? Your horse got spooked?”

She nodded, her quivering lips making it difficult to speak.

The deputy turned to his son. “Any of your friends fooling around with firearms?” The father cupped his son’s shoulder firmly. “If you guys aren’t careful, you’ll lose your hunting license.”

“We weren’t fooling around. I swear,” the young man complained.

The deputy turned to her. “Maybe it was a car back-firing.”

She shrugged and visibly shuddered.

"Let's get you home." Deputy Banks held out his hand, directing her toward his pickup truck.

Liddie turned to the son. "Are you sure you can handle this? Brownie's a little skittish after the loud noise."

The deputy's son smiled for the first time. "No problem." He hopped up into the buggy, then leaned over and grabbed the reins that had fallen during the accident.

Liddie was about to protest again when a stiff frigid wind finally forced her hand. She had no reason not to trust this kid and his father.

Once inside his truck, Deputy Banks turned up the heat full blast. Liddie held up her numb hands to the vents. The deputy pulled out onto the road and looked in his rearview mirror. "Don't worry. Carl's had a lot of experience with horses. We own three."

In the side mirror, Liddie angled her head to watch the deputy's son behind the reins of her buggy. *It'll be okay, Brownie*, she mentally telegraphed to her sweet horse as the buggy seemed to lurch forward before finally straddling the lanes on the country road.

A short while later, Deputy Banks turned in to the lane of the Troyer farm, then shifted toward her. "If it would make you feel better, I can call the incident in. A report of shots fired. Have one of the on-duty deputies check out the area."

Liddie's gaze drifted toward the house. The same warm light she had seen earlier when she and Elijah passed by still glowed in the front room. Jonah was up late. The thought of a patrol car coming out here unsettled her. She could check out Moses's information herself without getting the sheriff's department involved. No need to upset the children.

Liddie cleared her throat. "*Neh*, you're right. It was probably a car backfiring."

Jonah sat in the front room ostensibly going through some papers, but in reality, he had been rehashing his conversation with Maggie's sister, Ruthann. Would his children be better off in a family environment without all the constant drama? The last embers of the wood-burning fireplace died out one after the other, but he still wasn't ready to retire. Snowball was curled up on a pillow near his feet. He reached down and touched his head with the tips of his fingers.

Suddenly the dog's ears twitched, his head came up, then he jumped to his feet. His claws clacked on the hardwood floor as he made his way to the front door. A tingling started in the base of Jonah's head. Slowly, he rose to his feet. "What's wrong?" he asked, more than surprised he had resorted to talking to a dog.

Jonah moved to the window and peeked out; a truck idled in front of his house. He frowned and stepped away from the window so he wouldn't be seen. "What's that about, Snowball? Someone lost?" It didn't seem likely.

He was about to peek out the window again when the front door handle jangled, followed by a quiet knock. He furrowed his brow. He had already flipped the dead bolt, so he wasn't worried about anyone getting in, unless he let them. And he wasn't expecting anyone.

The knock sounded again, quiet, respectful.

"Who's there?" he asked through the door.

"It's Liddie."

Jonah scrambled to undo the lock and flung open the door, his gaze instinctively drawn to the truck behind her. "I didn't expect you..." His words trailed off as he took in her disheveled appearance. He stepped back to let her pass, shocked by her muddy dress. "What happened? I thought you were visiting your family."

Liddie lifted her weary gaze to him. She plucked the fabric of her wet dress away from her legs and said in an exhausted voice, "Can you please check on my horse? Deputy Banks's son is bringing her up with my buggy."

He studied her, trying to process what she was saying. "Of course. Of course. Are you okay?"

"*Yah, yah*... Let me change into dry clothes and I promise to tell you everything."

Jonah threw on his coat and ran out to the yard. Deputy Banks climbed out of the truck and took off his cap. "Good evening, Jonah."

"Evening." An uneasiness settled in Jonah's gut, like the moment just before a person was about to find out something they didn't want to know. He glanced back toward the house, wanting to allow Liddie the chance to explain before Banks had his say. He felt a certain sense of loyalty toward her.

"Seems your nanny can't stay out of trouble." Deputy Banks took a step toward him, tucking his hands into his pockets, and rolling up on the balls of his feet. Seemed the deputy was going to get the first word.

Out of the corner of his eye, Jonah saw the horse and buggy turn up the lane. "Let me take care of Liddie's horse."

"Ah, you can meet my son Carl."

The deputy followed Jonah over to the buggy. "Thanks." He had so many questions, but again, he wanted the answers directly from Liddie.

"Yeah, no problem," the kid said, as he slid over and

jumped down to the ground. He covered one fisted hand with the other and blew into them, obviously chilled from the ride. "I'm going to wait in the truck."

Jonah took the kid's place on the bench. The deputy hovered nearby, obviously eager to say something. "It's late, Deputy. I'm going to get the horse settled and call it a night."

The deputy took a step back and tipped his hat. "Night then."

Jonah flicked the reins and the horse jerked forward. He felt the deputy's eyes on him as he made his way toward the barn. He unhitched Liddie's horse and led her into the barn to an open stall. He ran a comforting hand down the neck of the strong animal. "Easy. Easy." The horse lifted her head and snorted, then seemed to settle in. He closed the gate, then slipped out of the barn, relieved to find the deputy and his son had gone.

Jonah hustled across the field, the hard, frozen earth crunching under each step. He went inside, took off his coat and boiled water for tea.

When Liddie finally appeared, she had her hair pulled into a long ponytail and was wearing sweatpants and a sweatshirt. She immediately apologized, apparently self-conscious about her attire. "I just needed to get warm," she whispered. "These are the warmest clothes I have." She plucked at the college sweatshirt. "And I figured the kids are sleeping. They won't see me." She rattled on.

He waved his hand, dismissing her *Englisch* clothes. He extended a mug of hot tea to her. "Let's sit by the fire." He threw in another log and poked it.

Liddie settled into the rocker across from his and seemed to sigh as she took a long sip of the tea. *"Denki."*

"You're welcome." He leaned forward, resting his elbows on his thighs. "Now please tell me what happened. I thought you were going to stay the night with your family." He found himself holding his breath, waiting for her to finally share her side of the story.

Liddie looked up toward the ceiling, then at him, her warm blue eyes sad. "My horse got spooked." She seemed lost in a trance. "I couldn't control her and I got tossed in a ditch."

"Are you okay?" He searched her face for any sign of injury. She seemed to be all in one piece. *Thank* Gott.

"I'm fine," she said, apparently wanting to dismiss that part of the story. "I shouldn't have been out alone."

Jonah ran a hand across his beard. "Back up. Start from the beginning. Why were you out so late?"

Liddie relayed the story about going to the bonfire with her brother in the hopes of asking questions about the man who had scared Daisy. About the man his daughter was convinced had hurt her mother.

"How do you know this man's friends?" Jonah asked. He didn't like the idea of Liddie hanging around Outsiders, especially ones who didn't appear to be upstanding citizens.

"Moses is Amish. He courted my sister for a bit, then he seemed to like me," Liddie said with a faraway quality to her voice.

"Do you like him?" The question fell from his lips before he had a chance to call it back. That really wasn't the point, but the thought made him feel something he hadn't in a very long time. Was he jealous? He shook away the thought. He had no business thinking along those lines.

"I have no interest in Moses," she said flatly. "I asked him what he knew about Dean."

Jonah waited, again getting that strange sensation that he wasn't going to like what he heard.

"Moses says that Dean and a few other guys had bragged about using unsuspecting farmers' land to grow marijuana."

Jonah's heart leaped to his throat. "Are they using my land?"

With both hands wrapped around the mug, she lifted it to her lips. She blinked slowly. She was obviously exhausted after tonight. "I don't know, but I think we should check." She reached over and placed the mug on the hardwood floor. "It would explain a lot, wouldn't it?"

"Did you tell the deputy?"

She shook her head slowly, then lifted her gaze to his. "It didn't feel right, him showing up right after Brownie got spooked. The noise sounded like a gunshot."

His eyes flared wide. "A gunshot? Do you think the deputy had something to do with it?" Had he taken aim at her? Cold icy dread hardened in his gut. Jonah had never cared for the deputy, but he had always attributed his unsettled feelings toward him to his role as investigator in his wife's murder.

"*Neh*, I don't think the deputy would hurt me." Liddie's face remained expressionless. "But it seems strange that his son was at the bonfire. The kid who brought the buggy home for me. The deputy told me he had just picked up his son." She shrugged and shook her head slightly. "Maybe I'm not thinking clearly."

"You did tell the deputy about the gunshot, though, right?"

"Yes, just not the information about the marijuana fields. No sense drawing any more attention to your farm than necessary, especially if I'm wrong."

"What did the deputy say about the gunshot?" Jonah asked.

"That it was probably a car backfiring." She let out a quick breath. "Maybe it was." She smiled slowly, but it didn't reach her eyes. "I really don't know. We need to check the fields for ourselves in the morning." She slowly got to her feet. "I'm tired."

Jonah wanted to reach out and take her hand and ask her a million more questions and at the same time reassure her that he'd protect her. But the traitorous words got lodged in his throat. Instead, all he said was, "Are you okay?"

"*Yah*, nothing a good night's sleep won't fix." She clutched her hands to her chest, as if she had sensed he had been close to taking one in his. "I better get to bed. The kids are up early."

TWELVE

Liddie rose with the sun and got ready for the day. As she was putting in the last pin to fasten her bun, she heard the floorboards outside her bedroom door creak. She placed her white bonnet neatly over her hair, leaving the strings dangling, and checked her reflection before slowly opening the door. Andy stood on one foot and had his arms extended out to his sides, balancing as if on a beam.

"New trick?" Liddie asked, unable to contain her smile. Leave it to a child to provide a welcomed reprieve from her worries.

Andy returned her smile and teetered precariously over to one side before righting himself. "*Yah*, Henry said he could do it longer than me, but next time I'm going to beat him."

Liddie reached out and tousled his hair. He needed to run a comb through it. "Did you have a nice visit with your cousins?"

He nodded eagerly. "I hope we can go back to visit. My aunt asked me if Daisy and I would like to live there, but I don't think there's enough room for all of us. *Dat* would miss his workshop."

Liddie wondered for a moment what that was all about, but she was too preoccupied with her own problems to take on any more. Already in hot water with her father, Liddie had made things worse by running off with her younger brother to a bonfire in the woods. She hadn't given her parents the courtesy of a goodbye. To add to her misdeeds, she had abandoned her drunk brother. She suddenly felt queasy. Her father would likely never forgive her.

Dismissing her growing dread, Liddie focused all her attention on the little acrobat. She playfully poked Andy's exposed ribs as he tried to balance on the opposite foot. When he started to tip, she grabbed his hand to steady him. A frown formed on his sweet face. Before he had a chance to protest, she whispered conspiratorially, "Want a surprise?" She needed to check on Licorice and Brownie. The little boy would be very excited to meet her horse.

His flash of frustration disappeared and was immediately replaced by an enthusiastic nod. His long bangs swooshed in his eyes, making him blink. "We're going to have to give you a haircut." She had often been charged with cutting her younger brothers' hair.

"Is that the surprise?" His shoulders slumped and he stuck out his lower lip, clearly disappointed.

"Do you think that's your surprise?" She laughed. "Of course not. Now, go get dressed because we're going outside and it might be a little chilly this morning. I'll meet you in the kitchen."

Once downstairs, she inspected her coat and groaned. Dried patches of mud clung to the fabric. Considering she had ended up in a ditch, she was amazed the entire coat wasn't ruined. She stepped out onto the back porch to flick off the dirt as best she could. It would need a proper washing later. She gave up and slipped her arms into the coat sleeves. She turned and stared out over the land. The early morning light reflected on the dew. The wind rustled through the overgrown land and the hairs on the back of her arms rose, giving her that uncomfortable "someone might be watching me" feeling again. Was someone really using Jonah's land without his knowledge?

"What's my surprise?" Andy's excited voice caught her off guard.

She spun around to find him standing in the doorway in his stocking feet. "Get your shoes and coat on and I'll show you." She held the screen door open. "Want help?"

"I'm a big boy." Andy dutifully listened and reappeared on the porch a few minutes later, black laces pooling around one boot.

Liddie bent down and tied it. When she straightened, the child had his cute face—reminiscent of his dad's—all scrunched up while he took in her coat. "Did you jump in the puddles?" he asked. "My *dat* doesn't like when I do that. I get muddy."

"I made a mess, didn't I?" She flattened her hand against the front of her coat and examined it. "It'll have to do for now because your surprise is waiting. Ready?"

"Ready!"

Liddie held up her finger in a hold-on-a-minute gesture and slipped inside to grab a few carrots and tucked them under the string of her apron to hide them from Andy and maintain the surprise. She took his hand and the two of them strolled across the yard. The subtle sensation that someone was watching her once again whispered across her neck, raising the fine hairs.

When they reached the barn, she hoped they'd find Jonah. She'd feel safer in his company. "Let's see if your *dat* is in the workshop." Liddie opened the latch and she was met with the sweet scent of pine and stillness. "Well, he's not here." She tried to sound playful even as the events of the past few days kept crowding in on her, making her jumpy. If only she could get out of her thoughts. If only she could have faith that things would be okay. "Let's go this way." She and Andy cut through the workshop to the other side of the barn to the horse stalls.

Liddie slowed as she grabbed the handle on the door to slide it open. "Ready?"

Andy nodded eagerly, his eyes focused on the door. Every interaction with Jonah's children made her heart grow fonder of them. Even after only this short time she couldn't imagine not being part of their lives.

Jonah's life.

"Hurry!" Andy said impatiently.

"Here." She reached between the flaps of her coat and grabbed two carrots. "You'll need these."

"The carrots better not be my surprise." He stared at them suspiciously and Liddie couldn't help but laugh.

"No, silly." She slid open the door separating the workshop from the stalls and Andy jerked his head back. "But they're a clue…" She let her words trail off.

Andy lifted the carrots, one in each hand. His eyes grew wide, a realization dawning. "Did we get a new horse?" He ran up to the stall door and held out one of the carrots to her horse Brownie.

"She's visiting for a little bit." Liddie opened the stall and sidestepped a few piles. She picked up the brush and ran it down the side of her horse. "How ya doing, girl?" She scanned the horse's coat for any injuries. "You don't look any worse for the wear, do you?" She let out a long breath of relief. She had worried about Brownie all night. The poor creature had really been spooked by the gunshot.

"Whose horse is this?" Andy said, scrunching up his face again.

"Mine. Her name is Brownie. I was allowed to name her when I was younger." Liddie had been very excited when her father suggested she name the beautiful brown foal. "Remember how I went to visit my family yesterday? Well, I wanted to come home, so I borrowed Brownie. My brother is going to stop by sometime to bring her home."

"You have a brother?"

"*Yah*, I have two brothers, Elijah and Caleb. Just like you are Daisy's brother."

The four-year-old seemed to be considering all this. "Why don't you live with them?"

"Long story." She smiled. "And not an interesting one like the books we read."

Andy glanced around, searching for something. "We need more carrots for Brownie and Licorice." His entire face lit up. "We need more! I'll get them."

He spun on his heel. She followed him to the door and watched him run toward the house, his muddy boots kicking up behind him. She wished she had his energy and enthusiasm.

"Where's he off to?"

Liddie turned to find Jonah approaching from the back fields. "To get more carrots. Apparently two horses need a lot of carrots."

Half of Jonah's mouth quirked up. Something about

the way he looked at her made butterflies flutter in her belly. "How are you this morning?" he asked.

"Fine." She swiped at her coat. "A little mud that should wash right out. And my hip ached a bit when I got up. But, really, I'm fine. Thanks for asking." She brushed the dirt from her palms and lowered her gaze, thinking about the cozy vibe that had lingered between them in the sitting room last night. She glanced into the barn toward the horses and she thought of a million different things she could say, but she finally settled on the most pressing. "Were you searching the property just now?" She had tried to remember if she had ever seen anything suspicious on her walks around the farm.

Jonah squinted at the sky with its first hint of pink and purple. "I was waiting for sunup." He took a step toward her. "I've been standing behind the barn, listening. Taking it all in." He shrugged. "I suppose I was also putting it off because I'm afraid of what I'll find. I couldn't sleep at all last night. If I discover someone was using this land for growing marijuana plants, it will be all my fault."

Liddie's heart went out to him. "It's not your fault," she whispered. "You couldn't have known."

He stared off into the middle distance. "If I had farmed the land like I had promised Maggie's family, I would have known, and none of this would have happened."

None of this. Like his wife's murder.

Liddie wanted to counter his argument, but she suspected her words would only ring hollow. Whatever they discovered today in the fields, ultimately Jonah would have to find a way to come to terms with it. To find peace within himself. No one could do that for him.

The front door creaked open and slammed shut. Andy raced back across the field with a carrot in each hand. "I have more carrots for Brownie." He held them up for his father and took big gulps of air. "Did you see Liddie's horse? Now Licorice has a friend." His excitement charged the air around him. "I'm so happy Liddie came to live with us. Aren't you happy, *Dat*?"

Liddie was amazed how an innocent question could make her feel all squirrelly. Out of the mouths of babes. Her eyes met Jonah's and held. A sly smile tilted the corners of his mouth. "*Yah*, I am happy that Licorice has a friend."

Liddie couldn't help but roll her eyes. Grateful for the levity, she turned to his son. "Let's go feed the carrots to the horses."

Andy's excitement about the horses had been a wonderful distraction from the dark thoughts that had kept him awake most of the night. Had his lack of attention to the land led to this evil? Could he have prevented all of this? The sickening thought dampened his appetite, despite the wonderful breakfast of cinnamon buns, bacon and eggs that his mother-in-law had prepared. At the first opportunity, he excused himself and headed back outside. He could no longer put off the inevitable, even if the truth was too painful.

He stepped off the back porch and heard the door creak behind him. Liddie smiled somewhat apologetically as she slipped outside and adjusted the lapels of her winter coat. She hunched her shoulders and scanned the horizon. "We've had a mild November, but it smells like snow."

"Smells like snow?" He tilted his head and studied her. "You have some odd ideas."

Liddie laughed. "Surely, you've smelled rain. Why can't I claim to smell snow?" She lifted her delicate hand and pointed to plump dark clouds floating in the distance. "Those are snow clouds."

"You didn't come out here to discuss the weather, did you?" Jonah said, impatient to head out into the fields now that he had worked up the nerve.

"Of course not. You weren't going for a walk—" she tilted her head, emphasizing her choice of words in case little ears were listening "—alone, now, were you? Ellen is finishing up in the kitchen and the kids are settled in the sitting room, so you're stuck with me."

Jonah opened his mouth to protest, then decided against it. Truth be told, he could use the company.

As they crossed the field, their teenage neighbor emerged from the path connecting the two properties with something in her hands. When she got closer, he could see it was a tray with a cloth draped over it.

"Guder mariye," Amity called to them, lifting the tray. "I brought some bread."

"Morning, Amity." Jonah drew in a deep breath. It was as if the world was conspiring against his plans to check the fields. "That was kind of you," he said, his polite response ingrained in him. "Are you sure your *mem* minds you bringing us this food? You've got a lot of mouths to feed over there."

"I love to bake and to share the fruits of my labor." Amity shrugged as if it were no big deal. "I can take this and put it in the kitchen. Are Mrs. Stolzfus and the kids inside?"

"*Neh*, we'll take it." He reached for the tray and Amity took a slight step back. *"Denki."*

"Oh, Liddie, what happened to your coat?"

"Nothing, just a little mud," Liddie said, also apparently in a hurry to get rid of the teenager. She extended her arms. "The children will love the treat."

"Actually, I was hoping to say hi to them, if that's okay," Amity pressed, making Jonah bristle. "Besides, I don't want to hold you up."

The teenager stared at them, apparently waiting for confirmation. Jonah wasn't about to reveal the real reason he and Liddie were about to explore the back fields on his property. There was enough gossip swirling around his family already, and he prayed Moses Lapp was wrong.

Jonah cut a quick glance at Liddie and she raised her eyebrows almost imperceptibly. "Sure, why don't we all go take the bread in." He felt compelled to join them for fear of seeming rude.

The three of them entered through the kitchen and Amity set the tray on the counter. "Hello, Mrs. Stolzfus," she said to his mother-in-law, who was drying the last pan from breakfast.

"Hello." The older woman tilted her head, acknowledging Amity's tray. "Looks like you've been baking."

The teenager smiled. "I have." She looked around hesitantly, as if waiting for an invitation. When one wasn't forthcoming, she said, "If you don't mind, I'd like to say a quick hello to the children." Without waiting for a response, Amity strolled into the sitting room and tousled Andy's hair. "Hello, everyone. I made some fresh bread."

Amity crouched down in front of Daisy, who was

sitting on the floor with her new constant companion. His daughter hugged her puppy tighter and seemed to recoil from their guest. Was she afraid Amity had come to reclaim the puppy?

"Now, now, Daisy," Jonah said from the doorway separating the kitchen from the sitting room. "Amity wants to say hello. You can't forget her generosity in giving you the puppy." His daughter looked up at him with those eyes that reminded him of his wife, and more times than not, broke his heart with their sadness. When she grumbled and tucked her face behind the puppy, Jonah sighed. "Daisy, stop being rude."

"It's okay, Mr. Troyer. I'm happy that Daisy loves Snowball." Amity picked up one of the children's books from the basket in the corner. "If you're headed out…" her gaze swept over Jonah and Liddie, both in their coats. "I could read to Andy and Daisy while you're gone."

Liddie seemed to have a refusal ready on her lips, but Jonah spoke up first. He'd rather have Amity inside with his children, than perhaps wandering out into the field behind them. If his worst fears were confirmed and someone had planted marijuana, he'd never be able to contain the rumors. "That would be fine. We won't be gone long."

Amity glanced down at the book, then as if mustering up the nerve, she asked, "Where are you going?"

"I want to show Liddie one of my new projects in the workshop." The white lie came too easily.

"Okay," she said, then to the children, "Who wants to hear a story?" Amity cheerily took a seat in the middle of the bench. She held out her arms to draw the children in.

Andy scooted up onto the bench next to her. "Me! I want to hear the story."

"How about you?" Jonah encouraged his daughter. "Don't you want to join your brother and Amity for a story?"

"I can hear from here," Daisy whispered, her voice soft as she stroked Snowball over and over, keeping her gaze fixed on some invisible dot in front of her on the hardwood floor. For every step forward they took with his sweet child, they seemed to take two back. Today Daisy seemed off. Perhaps she had overheard his and Liddie's conversation last night? The familiar hollowness in his chest expanded, reminding him that he failed more often than not at being a father. He needed desperately to protect his children.

"We'll be back shortly," Jonah said, unsuccessfully trying to catch Daisy's gaze. He opened the front door for Liddie and allowed her to step out onto the porch first. "I feel I'm not doing enough by Daisy," he said, keeping his voice low. "She should have minded me, but instead I let her stay on the floor with the puppy." His mouth twitched. "When I was growing up, we never let pets in the house. And we certainly minded our parents." Yet with a sickening dread he knew his concerns were much deeper than disobedience and rules.

"Daisy has been through a lot. You're doing a *gut* job." A warm smile brightened Liddie's blue eyes, and not for the first time he wondered how he had come to be blessed with her in their lives. They had all been blessed. "She answered you in a full sentence. It's far more than the nods I generally get."

A moment seemed to stretch between them before

he broke eye contact. "I'm sorry that Daisy has been rude to you."

"No, no, that's not what I meant. I just wanted to tell you that you're doing fine. In the short time I've been here, I've seen her coming out of her shell." A rush of breath rushed out of her nose. "Despite all the mayhem I've brought with me."

Jonah returned his gaze to hers. "I guess we're both good at blaming ourselves..." He let the words trail off and this time he didn't turn away. A small fissure cracked the wall he had built around his heart in the days and weeks and months—the year—since his wife's murder. He blinked, snapping himself out of the moment. A brisk wind whipped across the field, making the small wisps of hair float above her delicate neck. As if sensing his observation, Liddie flipped up her collar and pulled her coat tighter around her.

"Where should we start searching?" Liddie stepped off the porch and strode toward the overgrown fields behind the barn.

He cleared his throat and hustled to catch up. "I was thinking we should walk the perimeter first, then weave our way in." He glanced down at her boots. "It's bound to be muddy."

Liddie waved her hand down her coat, still partially caked with the mud from last night's accident. "I'm not afraid of a little dirt." Her pretty pink lips curved upward and humor sparkled in her eyes.

He couldn't help but return her smile. "Let's go then." As they headed toward the greenhouse, the short burst of levity disappeared. He'd have to finish tearing the structure down before it collapsed. "Even if someone did use my land, they may have already removed the plants this late in the season."

"*Yah*, maybe we should split up. Make the search faster."

"*Neh*, let's stick together." He palmed his felt hat and pushed it farther down on his head. He didn't want to leave Liddie out of his sight deep in the fields. "Do you know what you're looking for?"

"Not exactly. Do you?"

"I'll know if something doesn't belong."

By the time they found a wheelbarrow and clippers next to some dried-out plants that he strongly suspected were marijuana, the plump snow clouds had moved in, casting the land in ominous shadows. A chill raced up his spine and he stifled a shudder.

Moses Lapp had been right. People—perhaps Dean Johnson—had taken advantage of his inattention and used the land to grow marijuana plants. A rock formed in the pit of his stomach.

A gust of wind made the plants sway. Jonah reached out and ran his thumb across the leaf of the fragrant plant. Several had been cut down in their entirety and lay in wait. He lifted his head and searched the field. Had they spooked someone?

"Why didn't they harvest all of these?" Liddie asked, turning in circles, apparently wondering the same thing he had.

"Something stopped them." That horrible sense of being watched made his scalp prickle. "We need to head in and report this." The sound of a car on the country road whizzed by.

"They were smart. They're not far from the road, but far enough to keep the crop hidden," Liddie suggested.

The reality of the situation crashed down on him, making him hot under his coat. He let out a long sigh. “How could I have let this happen?” Jonah snatched up the clippers someone had left behind and began hacking away at the plants. “I should have never let this happen.”

“Jonah! Jonah! Stop! You didn’t cause this,” Liddie hollered. “Leave them. We have to notify the sheriff’s department.”

Jonah dragged a branch to the wheelbarrow and threw it on top. A sharp edge caught his palm and blood oozed out onto his dirty hand.

“Please, Jonah, stop.”

“What is the sheriff’s department going to do? Deputy Banks has been out here countless times yet look what’s here.” He paused and ran the back of his hand across his forehead. “He promised to patrol the area. Yet this goes on. Someone was out here recently with a wheelbarrow and clippers.” A muscle twitched under his beard and he stilled. “There’s no rain sitting in the wheelbarrow.”

“You have a lot of property. Whoever did this knew how to hide the crops.” Liddie took a step toward him and stumbled, then steadied herself and examined her boot that had sunk into the soft soil. “The sheriff’s department needs to question Dean Johnson. Moses told me this is exactly the type of thing he does.” She lifted her gaze and looked around him. “What if he comes back?”

Jonah picked up the clippers again and winced.

“Please, you need to get gloves. Your hand is bleeding,” Liddie persisted.

Jonah tossed the clippers aside on top of the downed

plants. "If rumors suggest Dean Johnson did this, then what about the man who killed Maggie?"

"He must not have been working alone," Liddie said in a soothing tone. His deep pain was evident on his face. "Please. Leave it be. We have to contact the sheriff's office."

Jonah let out a long, ragged breath and glanced around, taking specific note of his location.

"I've taken morning walks not too far from here." Her blue eyes widened slightly, as if just now coming to a realization. "Perhaps their attack on me was to scare me away. To stop me from stumbling upon—" she jabbed her hand in the direction of the dying plants—"this."

Jonah rubbed the back of his neck. "It's November. They'd almost cleared out of here." The wheelbarrow and clippers were evidence of that. "And we wouldn't have known."

Liddie frowned. "They may have had plans to return in spring."

Jonah's stomach bottomed out. How long had this been going on while his children played nearby in the yard? Unsuspecting. Unprotected. He had mistakenly thought that Oliver Applegate's arrest had been the end of the evil on his farm. He couldn't have been more wrong.

THIRTEEN

When Deputy Banks pulled up in his patrol car, Liddie's heart sank. She had hoped when Jonah called the sheriff's department that her friend, Deputy Bitsy King, would have responded. She supposed today was going to be one of those days where she couldn't catch a break. She had suggested to Jonah that they call Bitsy directly, but he had seemed intent on going through official channels. Perhaps he wanted Deputy Banks to know what he had neglected to find the multiple times he had been on Jonah's land. Because the deputy had often made clear his mild annoyance at being called out to his farm when the Amish, in general, rebuffed law enforcement. And it hadn't helped that the deputy had been the one who rescued her from the side of the road last night. He seemed to delight in finding fault. Liddie wondered if he had the same temperament with the *Englisch* he was called to serve.

The deputy climbed out of his patrol car and tipped his hat in her direction. Something flashed in his round eyes set deep in his full face. "Seem to be running into you a lot lately." An undercurrent of amusement that came as no surprise threaded through his comment.

Liddie's cheeks heated at the smarmy way he smiled at her. She didn't want to worry about what he thought about her, but she couldn't help it. He had found her on the side of the road after she had gone to the same bonfire as his son. Did he think she was a wild rule breaker?

"Thank you for helping me out last night," Liddie said, trying to relax her jaw while portraying the model of wholesome Amish living.

"How are you doing?" he asked.

"Fine." She smiled tightly.

"And your horse?"

"Seems to be fine, too. I appreciate that your son got her home for me. I'm not sure I properly expressed my gratitude last night. I had grown absolutely numb from the cold and couldn't wait to get inside to warm up." Liddie had decided to be gracious. "Did you have a chance to investigate?" She found herself holding her breath, waiting for the answer.

The deputy frowned. "The gunshot?" He surprised her with a quick nod in the affirmative. "Carl and I doubled back and I sent the spotlight into the trees. Didn't see anything out of the ordinary."

Liddie shrugged, not sure what to feel. "Maybe it was a car backfiring." She really didn't believe that. Not after everything else that had happened.

"I'll keep asking around." The deputy ran his hand over the back of his neck as the November sun beat down on him. "What's going on out here today?"

"I was the one who called," Jonah said, coming up behind her. "Seems someone is using my land to grow marijuana."

The deputy's bushy eyebrows drew down under the

shadow of his hat. "Someone? Why do I feel like you know more than you're saying?"

"Last night a friend of mine—" Liddie purposely left out Moses's name so as not to get him into trouble "—told me Dean Johnson has been known to use vacant land to grow weed."

"Dean Johnson again?" The deputy rubbed a hand across his jaw. "You have something against this kid?" The skepticism in his tone grated her nerves.

"I'm only telling you what I heard." Liddie did her best to hide her frustration.

"Is that why you went to the bonfire? To see what you could dig up?" His obvious condescension made her cheeks heat. "Funny how you never mentioned that when I pulled you out of the ditch."

"I asked around, yes," Liddie said, hiking up her chin, ignoring the dig.

"For a group of people who want to remain separate, you surely have our number on speed dial."

"We found the plants," Jonah said with a flat affect. Liddie worried that sweet man had become beaten down by all his troubles.

"Really?" The single word left no mistake about how the deputy felt. "I suppose you want me to go out and arrest this kid."

"We'll leave you and your *Englisch* laws to figure that out," Jonah said forcefully. "But for the safety of my family—" he held out his hand to encompass Liddie and something funny flickered in her belly "—this stops now."

The deputy held up his hands, a practiced gesture, Liddie imagined, from years of trying to get agitated people in stressful situations to settle down. "Show me what you found."

"This way." Jonah turned and strode toward the greenhouse, a man determined to take back his land. Liddie started to follow when a small sedan turned into the yard and bumped over the ruts. *Bitsy.*

Liddie stopped and waited for her friend to get out of her car.

"Hello there," Bitsy said. "I see Ed got here already."

Liddie shrugged and bit back what would have been a negative reply.

"I heard the call over the radio." Bitsy tugged on the zipper of her fleece jacket, pulling it all the way up to her chin. "What's going on? Everyone okay?"

Liddie released a breath she hadn't realized she'd been holding. The friendly deputy's presence had a calming effect. She brought the newcomer up to date, omitting the part about her accident, figuring that was a footnote, for now. Liddie balled her hands and pulled them up into the sleeves of her coat as a chill raced down her spine at the memory of the icy water at the bottom of the ditch. She cleared her throat. "Jonah and Deputy Banks are in the fields now. It's going to be a big job to yank all the plants."

"We can get some workers in to help," Bitsy suggested. "There's no reason Jonah has to do this. The sheriff's department is going to want to take the plants into possession and make sure they're properly disposed of."

Apparently sensing Liddie's unease, Bitsy said, "You've had a rough go of it, but I want you to know I'm on your side. Don't let anyone shame you into staying quiet, especially not Deputy Banks. He has a chip on his shoulder because we're charged with protecting all of the community. He resents that the Amish like to stay separate."

"It doesn't make things easy."

Bitsy shook her head slowly. "No, I suppose not. But your job isn't to make his easier. He has to learn to do all his duties, including protecting the Amish." The deputy tilted her head to force Liddie to meet her gaze. "Remember, I grew up Amish. I'm on your side. I know how it is."

Liddie smiled. "Thanks. It's not often I feel like I have someone on my side."

"Jonah's on your side."

"What?" Her defensive response slipped out before Liddie had a chance to call it back, embarrassment heating her cheeks.

Bitsy stepped closer and amusement sparked in her eyes. "I'm a very observant person. It's a requirement of the job. I've seen Jonah look at you like you mean the world to him."

"I don't. He had Maggie."

Bitsy reached out and touched Liddie's hand. "I had the pleasure of meeting Maggie a few times in town. Beautiful woman. She's in heaven now."

Liddie's ears burned.

Bitsy continued, "Jonah's still here. And so are you."

An awkward giggle escaped Liddie's lips and made her feel silly. "Why are you giving me matchmaking advice? Aren't you supposed to solve crimes?"

"That's my first job." Bitsy rubbed her lips together, apparently trying to suppress a smile. "Sometimes I like to throw in my two cents, even where it doesn't belong." She cleared her throat and grew somber. "Both of you have been through a lot and sometimes it's hard to see the forest through the trees."

Early the next morning, Liddie woke up and the rumble of thunder in the distance and the pelting of rain against the bedroom window made her roll over and pull the covers over her head. In the warm cocoon, she drifted back to sleep and dreamed that she and Daisy had gone for a walk behind the greenhouse. The midday sun beat down hot on them. The birds were chirping. As they walked and walked through the endless weeds, the clouds suddenly rolled in. It grew dark. Thunder rumbled.

Daisy turned and smiled up at Liddie, a genuine smile of a happy six-year-old. "Follow me," she said in the dream. She stepped backward between two nasty-looking, prickly weeds and disappeared. Liddie reached out and swiped at the plants. The thorns slashed at her flesh. The vegetation grew lusher, taller, pricklier, swallowing up every last bit of space. Swallowing up the little girl.

"Daisy!" Liddie's strangled, muffled cries woke her out of a fitful sleep. The sweet smell of French toast snapped Liddie back into the moment despite her racing heart and sweaty palms that made the nightmare feel so realistic. She ran her hand across her skin, reassuring herself that the nightmare thorns hadn't ripped her flesh apart. She let out a long breath of relief, grateful she had been dreaming.

Liddie flipped back the quilt and got ready for the day. The plans to clear the fields would probably be hampered by the weather. Downstairs, she found Ellen stacking the French toast on a plate. "Morning," Liddie said. The house felt eerily quiet. "Is everyone still sleeping?"

"The children are. Jonah is out in the workshop."

Of course.

"Can I help you?" Liddie asked automatically, surprised when Ellen held out her hand toward a melon.

"If you don't mind."

"Not at all," Liddie said, pleased. The elderly woman had shut her out of the kitchen since she had arrived. She grabbed a knife from the block and began to slice the fruit. The sweet smell reached her nose and made her stomach rumble.

"I've been thinking about a lot of things," Ellen said, making Liddie pause mid cut. She could only imagine what the elderly woman was going to say next. "A lot has been going on here since you arrived."

Liddie wondered how much Jonah had shared with his mother-in-law and she didn't want to overstep and worry the woman. She had already been through so much with the murder of her daughter.

Ellen glanced over her shoulder, as if to make sure little ears wouldn't overhear. "Jonah told me about the marijuana plants."

"The sheriff's department said they'd take care of them," Liddie said, feeling as if she somehow owed this woman an apology.

Ellen stopped what she was doing and turned to face Liddie, resting her hip on the counter. Liddie set the knife aside to give the woman her full attention. "My husband and I had a chance to sell this land, but we didn't want to let it go. We wanted the next generation to raise their children here. So, we asked Maggie and Jonah to come back to Hickory Lane to take care of the land. To take care of us." Ellen pushed off the counter and laced the dish towel through the handle on the cabinet. She kept her back turned momentarily, apparently gathering her thoughts, or perhaps her emotions. "Jonah never had any interest in farming." She slowly turned around. "We let all this land go to waste. I feel like..." The woman's voice warbled.

"I think it's human nature to question your choices. I imagine your husband was happy to spend his final days on the land where he had raised his family," Liddie said, hoping to bring this woman some comfort.

Ellen got a faraway look in her eyes. "Yes, but this land was all too much for him."

"*Gott* has a plan."

Ellen sighed and her shoulders sagged. "My eldest daughter is mad we didn't offer the land to them. She has a big family." She pressed her work-worn hand to her neck. "I thought they were settled on their own land. It was Jonah and Maggie who seemed like they needed our help more. What with Jonah off building those fancy homes. It's not right for a man to have to leave his home to find work. We thought our farm would be the answer for them. My husband and I had a *gut* life here."

"Jonah's doing his best."

Ellen watched her a beat, not indicating if she agreed or not. "On Sunday, I overheard Ruthann, my oldest daughter, telling Jonah that her family could take over the farm since he wasn't using it."

Liddie's entire body tensed. "Is there enough room for Jonah and Ruthann's family here?" Selfishly the one question that screamed at her, but she didn't dare voice was, "Where does all this leave me?" Her cheeks heated at the selfishness of her worry.

Ellen pulled out a chair at the kitchen table and sank into it. "Ruthann offered to raise Daisy and Andy. She suggested they'd be happier as part of a big family." The children's grandmother looked up with tears in her eyes. "My own daughter suggested Jonah give up his children. That he get an apartment in Buffalo close to his work."

Liddie's heart broke. "Jonah's not…" She couldn't even say the words. He'd never leave his children.

Ellen shook her head. "*Neh, neh*... How could my own daughter be so cruel to Jonah, her sister's widower?"

"I'm sure she didn't mean to be." Liddie defended the stranger, if only to bring comfort to Ellen.

The older woman waved her hand. "I haven't been able to sleep worrying about this. I know Ruthann blames Jonah for not being here to protect Maggie. And I've been curt to you because I'm upset my daughter isn't here to raise her own children. It's a very cruel cycle."

"We all need someplace to focus our negative energy." Liddie smiled tightly, studying the top of Ellen's bonnet as the woman bowed her head seemingly in grief.

Ellen looked up, her lips trembling. "I've been focusing mine on you and I'm sorry." She ran the tips of her fingers nervously back and forth over the edge of the table. "Will you forgive me?"

"Of course." Liddie wrapped her hands around the edge of the counter to steady herself.

"You've been good for the children. And Jonah."

At the mention of Jonah, Liddie felt her face flush. Ellen continued, "He spends more time with them because of you. Before you arrived, he withdrew from all of us. I suppose he was mostly avoiding the memory of Maggie." A shy smile creased her face. "I suspect this change is due to you. He seems to enjoy your company."

"I'm the children's nanny. He spends time with me out of necessity." Ellen's observation on the heels of Bitsy's comments made Liddie's knees go weak. Had she been too naive to see what was right in front of her? *Neh*, she hadn't known Jonah very long. She was here for his children. Not him.

"I have a feeling you're too hard on yourself," Ellen said, interrupting her train of thought. "Perhaps *Gott* has brought you here for a reason."

The sound of heavy feet grew closer and Andy appeared with a book in his hand. "Can you read to me, Liddie?" She had never been more grateful for an interruption.

"Isn't that the book Amity read to you yesterday?" Liddie took the book and turned it over in her hands. "You must be tired of it by now."

"She didn't read to me." The mild disgust in his tone suggested he was mimicking the adults in his life.

"No?" Liddie said, curiosity prickling her scalp.

Daisy drifted into the kitchen, as if she had been waiting for her cue from the other side of the wall. "*Yah.* She's very nosy. She stood at the window the whole time." She heavily emphasized the word *whole*.

Liddie bit back a reprimand, thrilled that Daisy was opening up to her even if she was being critical of Amity. There didn't seem to be any love lost between Daisy and the teenaged neighbor. Perhaps Daisy feared she'd take back the puppy. "Amity has been very nice to you." Something about the teenager spying out the window rubbed Liddie the wrong way, but she didn't want to say as much in front of the children.

Daisy quickly looked down at her feet. Liddie crouched down in front of her and touched her arm. "Is there something you're not telling me?"

The girl's expression grew shuttered and she shook her head tightly. If Liddie hadn't been watching her so closely, she might have missed the flash of fear on Jonah's daughter's face.

"Honey?" Liddie coaxed.

"I wanted to hear the story," Andy interrupted, apparently feeling like now was a good time to vent his grievances among his supporters.

Liddie gently squeezed Daisy's arm in a show of support. "I suppose I can read it to the both of you now. Unless your grandmother has more for me to do."

Ellen smiled. "I believe I have everything under control." This time, her words held a bit of humor and Liddie was grateful that she had finally broken the ice with the children's grandmother. The idea that Ellen might be playing matchmaker both horrified Liddie and warmed her heart. The conflicting emotions twisted and wound their way around her chest, making it difficult to draw in a decent breath. How could her boss—Daisy and Andy's father—court her? What would that even look like? And what if it went bad? Liddie didn't want to jeopardize her position, or more importantly, her relationship with these precious children.

Butterflies of romantic anticipation turned into a sour taste in her mouth. What exactly had Amity been looking for out the window?

Liddie shoved the spiraling thoughts aside and ushered the children into the sitting room and onto the bench. She had gotten halfway through the book when she heard Jonah entering through the mudroom where he discarded his raincoat.

Ellen called the children into the kitchen and Jonah pulled Liddie off to the side where the children couldn't overhear. "Deputy Banks called me this morning on my work phone."

Liddie felt her heart racing in her ears. "Oh." The single word came out as a squeak.

"Dean Johnson seems to have gone missing."

"What do you mean? Missing?"

"He's not home and his mother claims he hasn't been there in over twenty-four hours. The deputy assures me they'll bring him in for questioning once they locate him."

Liddie's eyes drifted toward the icy rain pelting the window. A chill raced down her spine that had nothing to do with the wicked weather outside.

FOURTEEN

Jonah was never a big fan of hunting or guns, never mind bringing a weapon into his home. All the same, after taking off his coat, he stashed his shotgun in the corner of the pantry and stored the bullets in the kitchen cabinet next to the coffee. Until whoever was using his land was in custody, he needed to protect his family.

The weather outside was fierce. The wind howled and the freezing rain had turned to windswept snow, pelting him as he crossed the yard from the barn. The only perk of winter was the additional time he could spend in his workshop. Other than that, he'd trade these freezing temperatures for a warm summer day in a heartbeat.

Jonah had already checked on both horses, making sure they had blankets to get through the frigid night. No one had come from the Millers' to pick up Brownie, and he suspected with the inclement weather, they wouldn't be coming any time soon. The cold seeped into every inch of his being as he swiped the water droplets from his beard. He couldn't wait to settle in next to the fireplace and warm his weary bones. He doubted he'd get any sleep. Not until Dean was brought in for questioning. The kid might be innocent, who knew? Yet, none of this felt right.

Jonah double-checked the lock on the back door. On his way through the kitchen to check the front door, he saw Liddie come down the stairs. "The children were tired. I think Andy was asleep the minute his head hit the pillow," she said.

"The dreary weather makes us all tired." Yet, despite being physically tired, he was mentally wide awake. Deep down, he sensed something awful was about to happen. He felt like he was in a storm, danger and mayhem lashing him like the icy snow with no place to escape.

"Is Ellen asleep?" Liddie asked. His mother-in-law's bedroom was on the first floor in the back of the house.

He glanced in that direction. He didn't notice the soft glow of a lamp creeping out from under the door. "Seems that way."

Liddie wrung her hands and rocked back on her heels.

"Calling it a night?" he asked.

She let out an awkward laugh. "*Neh*, I'm afraid I'd be staring at the ceiling all night. You?"

"I was going to make myself some tea. Join me? We can sit by the fireplace."

"I'd like that." She brushed past him into the kitchen. "Let me get the tea." She tipped her head toward the wood-burning fireplace. "You'll need to stoke the fire."

Jonah felt compelled to tell her he'd get the tea. A kind gesture to let her know he appreciated her. A flutter in his gut took him back to the days when he was first courting his wife. He thought he'd never feel this way toward anyone else. Yet, slowly but surely, this young woman had worked her way into all of their hearts.

His gaze drifted to the fire. She was right. He'd have to toss on another log. She was proving herself to be a very smart woman. A good influence on his children. Ellen had even warmed up to her. "I'll grab a few more logs from the porch."

Bracing against the cold, he went outside and closed the door behind him. A wicked gust of wind slapped him in the face. "Oh, man." He grabbed a few logs off the top of the woodpile and adjusted the vinyl cover. Wet wood wouldn't do them any good to ride out this storm.

Balancing the wood in one arm, he reached for the door handle when it flew open. He was met with Liddie's pretty smile glowing in the soft lamplight. "Thought you might have your arms full." The warmth in her eyes melted his heart.

He couldn't help but smile in return. She held the door open for him and he brushed past her. She smelled flowery, like lavender maybe. His cheeks warmed at the thought and he turned away, grateful that he had to stack the wood in the rack. He tossed the driest piece on top of the fire. He poked the wood and embers sparked and the flames were roaring once again before he sat down in a rocker to enjoy the cozy heat.

A few minutes later, Liddie came out of the kitchen with two mugs and set his down on the table between the two rockers. Liddie sat down, stared at the fire for a bit and was the first to break the companionable silence. "I loved snowstorms when I was growing up. It was one of the only times I was allowed to sleep in."

Jonah smiled. "Weren't there still chores to do?" That

was the part about farming that he didn't like. The work was constant. Working construction had a stop and start time. And a steady income. Two reasons he had been reluctant to take over the farm, but ultimately his wife had convinced him to move here, at least. And now with everything falling apart around them, Ruthann was trying to sway him to give up the land once and for all.

"Yes, but my father did the chores on those mornings." The nostalgia in Liddie's soft voice soothed him. "He never seemed to mind the cold. He'd let us kids sleep in, which really wasn't that long because we were so excited about being able to sleep in." She laughed quietly. "Then we'd go downstairs and the girls would help *Mem* make cinnamon rolls and the boys would run out to play in the snow and *Dat* would rope them into mucking out the horses' stalls anyway. It was a masterful plan." He followed her gaze to the window, the snow invisible beyond the reflection of the light in the glass. "Snowstorms always seemed to bring us together. Just a bit of a change in the schedule to make us pay attention."

"Life does have a way of getting into a routine and we forget to appreciate what's right in front of us."

Liddie fixed her gaze on his and he felt a spark between them. He cleared his throat and changed the subject. "It seems you and Ellen have come to an understanding." He noticed the tension between them had eased.

Liddie took a long sip of her tea. "She's finally letting me help in the kitchen."

He picked up his mug, then set it back down. "Is that a good or bad thing?"

Liddie laughed. "*Gut.* I don't mind." He couldn't take

his eyes off of her face. In this light, she looked striking. She bit her bottom lip, as if carefully measuring her words. "She told me that the children's aunt wants this farm."

Renewed anger washed over him at the nerve of his former sister-in-law. "Did you hear that she also wants the children?" A quiet gasp escaped Liddie's mouth, but he plowed on. "She thinks she can move right in. That I'll just leave them with her." He scrubbed a hand over his face. "Once word gets out that someone was growing marijuana on this land without my knowledge, she'll press her case. Insist that it's best for everyone if she and her husband take over the farm." His breath came out on a jagged sigh.

Liddie reached out, but stopped short of touching his hand. "She cannot do anything without your approval. And Ellen doesn't want you to go. You know that, right?"

His jaw twitched and he turned to face her. He didn't know anything. Not for sure. An aching hollowness expanded in his chest. "Do you think my kids would be better off growing up in a big family with all their cousins?" He turned away and rested his head on the back of the rocking chair. "You should see them when they're at their cousins'. It's an entirely different atmosphere. They're happy." He cleared his throat, afraid of the emotion that was welling up inside him.

"Of course they're happy around their cousins. Who wouldn't be? Don't you remember packing up to visit family? Children love having other children around."

Jonah nodded, his thoughts drifting to long afternoons running around the pond with his four brothers and their cousins who lived on a nearby farm.

"More importantly," Liddie said, her soothing voice a calming balm for his restless spirit. "Your children need you." Genuine sincerity glistened in her eyes in the firelight. "Children need their father." Her somber expression grew playful and she waggled her finger at him, an apparent attempt to lighten the mood. "Don't get any silly ideas just because their aunt has her eye on a bigger farmhouse."

Jonah couldn't help but laugh. "You're *gut* for the children."

She lifted a shoulder, and a self-deprecating expression swept across her delicate features. "I try."

Jonah shifted in his seat and searched her face. Something inviting in her eyes gave him the courage to reach out and brush his knuckle across her cheek. Her skin was smooth and warm. She lowered her gaze, her long lashes leaving a shadow on her cheeks in the flickering light. After a pause, she lifted her eyes to meet his steady gaze.

Jonah wasn't sure if it was the storm blowing outside, or the warmth inside, but he felt like they were the only ones in the world. Resting his elbow on the arm of the rocker, he leaned in closer to her. When she didn't back away, he placed his lips on hers, soft and warm. After the briefest of moments, he pulled away and whispered, "You're good for me, too."

Liddie woke up the next morning and found herself feeling a little bit shy after Jonah's kiss last night. Maybe it had been the close confines by the fire. Maybe it had been the storm roaring outside, or the one within, but she had let down her guard. They both had.

His words, "You're good for me, too," floated through

her mind all night. What did this mean? As soon as he had said it, she quickly diverted the conversation back to the children and how much she had grown to care for them. Jonah had assured her the feeling was mutual. Then she gathered up their mugs, set them in the kitchen and said good-night. Now, she'd have to face him this morning. Would he regret his confession?

Would she?

Shoving the thoughts aside, she rushed to get ready for the day and headed downstairs, bracing herself as she reached the bottom of the stairs, then sighing in relief when she found the kitchen empty at this early hour. Maybe she could get some coffee and confidence before she had to see anyone, especially Jonah. Her face flushed all over again at the memory of the tickle of his beard brushing against her chin. His soft, warm lips. What had she been thinking last night? How would she ever face him this morning?

She filled a kettle with water and glanced out the window over the sink—where their mugs from last night sat—and was amazed to see the deep snowdrifts. Even in Western New York, November was early for a storm of this magnitude. Deep tracks led from the house to the barn. Jonah must have gone out to feed the horses. She wondered how long ago he had slipped out. How long before she'd have to face him. What could he possibly be thinking about her this morning? Inwardly she groaned to herself.

She hurriedly set the kettle on the stove and turned on the gas. She could offer him hot coffee to warm up the minute he came in. She could act like nothing had happened. She could start breakfast. Take care of the children. Do the job she had been hired to do.

Avoid him.

She let out a long sigh and leaned back against the counter and gingerly touched her lips and closed her eyes. The anxious whisper that encouraged her to pack her bags and move out so she'd never have to face him again was shushed by a realization that the emptiness she had often felt inside didn't feel so hollow this morning. Her growing relationship with Jonah and his family had everything to do with that. But what if they had a falling-out? Where would that leave the children? She couldn't bail on them. They needed her.

The tendrils of warmth wound tight and her stomach began to hurt. Why did she overthink everything? Perhaps because she had made too many mistakes in her life. She didn't want to make a monumental one that would hurt these sweet children, especially Daisy who needed consistency.

Feet stomping across the floor grew closer. She opened her eyes and found Andy racing toward her, as if summoned out of her darkest worries. His hair was mussed and she resisted reaching out and touching his cowlick, the same one his father had.

"It snowed! It snowed!" Andy jumped up and down, his fists pumping. "Can we go out and play?"

"Well..." Liddie couldn't help but smile at his excitement. "We need to eat first because playing in the snow takes a lot of energy." She opened a cupboard. "Maybe I could start breakfast." She and Ellen had come to an understanding of sorts and Liddie no longer worried about stepping on the older woman's toes in the kitchen. "How would you like pancakes?"

"Neh, neh, neh." Ellen appeared in the doorway, tying her apron around her waist.

Liddie clasped her hands in front of her. "Oh, I didn't mean..." The familiar dread of offending the children's grandmother sparked, then immediately flickered out when she noticed the twinkle in the older woman's eyes.

"We always have cinnamon buns the morning after a snowstorm. Andy, go get on warm clothes and I'll make breakfast." Ellen bustled into the kitchen, effectively pushing Liddie aside and busying herself with dough preparations. Liddie finished making a cup of instant coffee and leaned against the counter mesmerized by Ellen kneading the dough in quick, efficient movements. "We used to make cinnamon buns the morning after a snowstorm, too, when I was growing up." This house was beginning to feel more and more like home.

"Then I suppose you should help me." Ellen flashed her a bright smile. "Grab the cinnamon." A command. Not a question. The woman was obviously not going to slow up her process for idle chatter. "You'll find it in the pantry."

"Of course." Liddie opened the pantry and searched the cans and boxes lined up neatly. Her eye was drawn to the floor and her heart stuttered when she noticed the shotgun. It hadn't been there before, had it? She drew in a shaky breath, a wave of fear threatening the peaceful morning. Jonah had been worried enough to bring the shotgun he usually kept in his workshop into his home.

"What's taking so long? It's in the rack on the door."

Liddie tore her attention away from the gun and turned. The spices were neatly lined up in a rack hanging on the back of the door. She plucked out the bottle of cinnamon.

Ellen had moved to rolling out the dough. "How did

you sleep last night?" A seemingly innocent question as she kept her entire focus on the task in front of her.

"Fine," Liddie said automatically when in reality, she had lain in bed staring up at the ceiling, listening to the storm howling outside and replaying that kiss. But now she couldn't stop thinking about that gun.

"I don't think I slept a wink. The wind was really howling."

"It was," Liddie said, noncommittally.

"What time did you go to bed? I heard you and Jonah talking." Ellen stopped rolling the dough and cut her a sideways glance, a twinkle of something in her eye that Liddie was reluctant to read too much into. "The wind kept me up and I promise I wasn't trying to eavesdrop." She reached over and patted Liddie's hand, leaving white flour prints. "You're good for this family."

Everyone seems to think so.

Then Ellen went back to rolling the dough and Liddie wanted to melt into the floor.

The sound of an exterior door opening and closing snapped Liddie back into the moment.

"Is that Jonah?" Ellen asked with a sly smile. This was an entirely new side of the woman that Liddie had never seen. She was sure she'd enjoy it more if the knowing gazes weren't directed at her.

"I don't think..." Since Jonah usually came through the back mudroom, Liddie rushed through the sitting room. The front door was open a gap, the arctic air rushing in. She pulled it all the way open and spotted Daisy outside with the quilt from her bed wrapped around her. She stood on the porch in thick socks while the appropriately named Snowball bounded across the snow-covered grass, sinking lower than his belly.

"Oh, honey! Come inside. It's too..." Her words trailed off when out of the corner of her eye, she spotted Dean Johnson on the rocker on the porch. Liddie's heart plummeted. On the surface, he seemed harmless enough, save the menacing expression on his face.

"Daisy," Liddie called, her voice trembling as she extended her hand. She now recognized the terror in the girl's eyes. Daisy was just out of her reach. Her fear made her impervious to the bone-chilling cold. "Daisy, sweetheart, come inside."

Daisy shook her head slowly and her jaw trembled. "He told me to stay here. He'll hurt Snowball."

Liddie glanced at the barn, praying that Jonah would see what was happening.

"Listen to me, Daisy. Come here!" Liddie's voice sounded surprisingly stern while her knees threatened to buckle under her. Dean stared back at her, a hint of amusement twinkling in his glossy eyes while something darker lurked in their depths. Her precious little girl stayed rooted in place.

Please, Gott, *help us.*

"Daisy, go inside now!" Liddie reached out and grabbed the girl's arm and tugged her, but Daisy fell to the floor into an unmovable blob. The girl's face crumpled. Liddie had never raised her voice to the child and she immediately regretted it. She needed the girl's cooperation, not her tears. Not her resistance.

Just beyond Daisy, Snowball bounded farther away from the house. There was no way Liddie could get the puppy and Daisy into the house before Dean did whatever he came here to do. Liddie doubted the dog was the only thing he meant to hurt. She drew in a deep breath, then stepped fully out onto the porch, between Daisy and Dean. The wind whipped at her skirt and the frigid air assaulted her legs.

A wolfish grin spread across the man's face. "You think you can stop me?"

Liddie held up her hands. "I don't know what you want. Just leave us alone."

"That's all I ever wanted. To be left alone." Menace sparked in his eyes under a black snow cap pulled low.

The freezing temperature was quickly making her face go numb, making it hard to form any words, but he seemed oblivious to the cold. "We don't want any trouble. Please leave." Her words came out garbled.

Dean slowly rose from the chair. The rocker swung back and hit the wall. Liddie didn't budge. Neither did Daisy. The little girl sat terrified, determined not to abandon her oblivious puppy. The smell of stale beer lingered on Dean's breath as he grew closer. "You took something that was important to me. Now, I'm going to take something that's important to you."

"You're not taking anything." Liddie lifted her chin in defiance, terrified he meant to take Daisy, too. "Go on in the house, Daisy. Now!"

"Snowball—"

"Now!" Liddie hollered, praying Daisy would be startled into obeying.

Daisy struggled to her feet. Dean charged Liddie, knocking her to the floor. She landed with an *oof*, the air escaping her lungs. Barely missing Daisy. Dean hovered over her, one solid boot on either side of her hips. "I should have killed you when you first came sniffing around." He reached down and dug his bony fingers into her arm, taking her immediately back to the day someone—no, *he*—had dragged her across the field when she had gone in search of Andy's ball.

Keep him talking. Maybe giving Daisy time to escape inside. She strained to locate her, but couldn't see around his hulking form.

"Were you the one who shot at me? Ran me off the road?" The cold, wet snow seeped into her clothing as she lay sprawled on the porch.

A shadow of pure anger raced across his face. "It was dark and I had too much to drink." Still straddling her, he crouched down and tapped her forehead with his meaty index finger. "Otherwise you'd be dead."

Liddie swallowed hard.

Dean straightened and stepped over her. He grabbed Daisy by the arm. "This one knows what I can do."

Liddie's heart dropped as she rolled onto her side to get a better view of Daisy. The poor girl whimpered in absolute terror.

"Where's your dolly?" Dean seemed to be talking to Daisy, but he didn't take his eyes off Liddie. "It was a shame her prized possession landed in a mud puddle, wasn't it?"

"That was you? You snatched Daisy and locked her in the neighbor's barn." With adrenaline surging through her veins, everything went into sharp contrast as she slowly got to her feet. She wanted to ask why he had taken Daisy, but it turned out, she didn't have to.

Dean was very chatty today.

"Thought maybe you'd get fired if Jonah thought you were a lousy nanny. With you gone, one less person snooping around my business." He patted his chest as if he were looking for his cigarettes. "Turns out this one knows how to keep her mouth shut." Liddie took a step toward Daisy. To protect her. But Dean was faster. He shoved Liddie hard and she landed on her backside. He scooped up Daisy and tossed her over his shoulder in a fireman hold. The poor girl screamed as he jumped off the porch with her.

Liddie blinked away the blurriness from getting the wind knocked out of her. "No!" she screamed. Dean turned around to taunt her, his progress hampered by the snow. He was heading toward the barn with lumbering steps. Pushing against the pain, Liddie rolled onto all fours, then pushed to her feet. She'd never be a match for him physically. She turned and raced into the kitchen, surprised Ellen hadn't heard the commotion.

"What's going on?" Deep worry lines creased the corners of Ellen's eyes.

"Stay inside." Liddie gulped in a deep breath. "Protect Andy." She snagged the shotgun from the pantry, ignoring her body aches.

"What's going on?" Ellen repeated, her voice growing agitated as she followed Liddie back through the sitting room.

"I want to go outside, too!" Andy hollered.

"Stay here with your grandmother. Do not come outside!" Liddie didn't slow down to register his shocked surprise. "You must do as I say." She gave a quick nod to a suddenly frail-looking Ellen, then ran back out onto the porch and slammed the door closed behind her. Panic made her nauseous and for the briefest of moments, she didn't know if she could do this.

Dean's progress across the yard had been hampered by the deep drifts. Snowball was yipping at his heels, at times disappearing completely in the snowdrifts.

From her perch on the porch, Liddie screamed across the field, "Stop!"

To her surprise, Dean stopped outright and turned toward her, perhaps ready to mock her. But—she couldn't be certain from this distance—she thought his eyes went wide when he saw the shotgun. There was no one she could risk hurting Daisy. Powered by adrenaline, Liddie stepped into the snowy field and trudged after him, her boots slicing through the snow. Instead of running away, he braced himself and eased Daisy off his shoulder and into his arms. The girl wept silently and went still, watching Liddie with a different kind of concern in her round eyes.

"Trust yourself with that thing?" Dean asked, struggling to position Daisy's body in a way that wouldn't even remotely block his large frame.

Liddie lifted the shotgun to her shoulder and steadied it with both hands. She closed one eye and aimed it at his forehead. "Try me. Unlike you, I'm as sober as the day is long."

FIFTEEN

Jonah had navigated his way through the freshly fallen snow to the barn. Didn't matter the weather, the animals still had to be fed. He didn't mind; he needed the fresh air to clear his head. He hadn't slept much. Multiple times throughout the night, he found himself wandering the quiet house he had once shared with Maggie. Back then, he'd pace, wondering how he was going to manage such a large farm, finally settling on keeping his reliable construction job instead. Last night, he had strolled the same cold floors determined to keep his family safe.

Liddie had filled his thoughts, too. He had grown close to the children's nanny, and he couldn't shake the feeling that he was being unfaithful to his deceased wife.

"What do you think, Brownie?" He patted Liddie's horse's nose. "You like it here, girl?" The horse lifted her nose and puffs of white vapor came out on a snort of approval. "Good thing. Because with this weather, I'm not sure anyone's coming to get you anytime soon." He stepped into the stall and found himself humming as he adjusted the blanket over the horse. "We'll make sure you're well taken care of."

His stomach growled and he found himself thinking ahead to breakfast. Actually, he found himself looking forward to the entire day cooped up in the house. He couldn't recall the last time he felt this way. He'd get to spend it inside with the children and their grandmother. And Liddie. Perhaps with the children around, they wouldn't have to feel awkward after their late-night kiss. Her pretty face floated to mind. He was done for.

In the adjacent stall, Licorice neighed, seemingly startled by something. He went over to the stall to check on the other horse. Licorice seemed to want to get out of her stall. "Easy, easy," Jonah said as he ran both hands down her side. "What's got you spooked?"

Just then, the wind carried in a shout of some sort. *Stop!* Was something going on at the neighbor's? Licorice lifted her nose and neighed. "Easy now." A whisper of dread made the hairs on the back of his neck prickle.

The children. Liddie...

Jonah secured the stall and rushed to the barn door and peeled it open. A gust of wind assaulted him. He stepped out onto the snowy field and his heart dropped. Liddie had his shotgun aimed at someone. A large man. His back to Jonah. The man shifted and Jonah saw his daughter dangling in his grip.

No one was going to hurt his family. Not now. Not ever. Not again.

How had Liddie known his shotgun was in the house? Thank *Gott* she had grabbed it.

He stepped back into the barn and glanced around. For something. A weapon of his own. He grabbed the pitchfork used for mucking the stalls and raced across the snow, following the tracks that he had made on the way to the barn. Trying to quiet his panting from exertion and fear, he came up behind the man. "Put my daughter down," he demanded, enunciating each word as anger and terror and rage and a million other emotions sent hot blood roaring through his veins.

The man slowly turned around. *Dean Johnson.* The start of a sly smile fell from the man's lips as Jonah swung the pitchfork, bringing it down hard across his head. His beloved Daisy, her scrunched up face expressing all the emotions she couldn't voice, slipped from his grasp and crumpled into the soft snow. Dean fell backward, landing with a puff of white that partially covered his face. Snowball bounded up and yapped at the man, inches from where he had fallen. He was out cold.

Jonah tossed aside the pitchfork and approached Dean and searched his face for any signs of consciousness. Cautiously, he patted the man's coat until he found his cell phone. He scooped up Daisy and held her close. "Are you okay?"

Daisy nodded into his chest. Then she pulled back her tearstained face and whispered, "We have to get Snowball." Her lips trembled from fear and the cold. "He's freezing."

A strangled cry of relief escaped his throat.

Liddie ran over, her pace slowed by the deep snow. She held the shotgun down by her side. He reached out and took it from her in exchange for the cell phone. "It doesn't appear to be locked. Go, go inside. Call the sheriff's department. I'll watch over him."

"Is the bad man who hurt Mommy dead?" Daisy asked, her wide eyes taking in the man splayed faceup in the snow, a trickle of blood snaking down from his hairline.

Jonah hated that his daughter had witnessed this. That she may have witnessed his wife's murder.

Why hadn't he believed her?

"He's never going to hurt anyone again, Daisy. I promise," Jonah said, as he handed her off to Liddie. "Can you carry her? She doesn't have any shoes on."

Liddie nodded, her lower jaw quivering. "You're safe now," she said as she grabbed his daughter. "Let's get you inside."

Jonah's fingers grew numb and the bone-deep cold made his entire body hurt. Dean Johnson lay unconscious in the snow, but based on the subtle flickering of his eyelids, he was about to come around. How easy it would be to end this miserable man's life. Stomp on his exposed neck. *Neh*, not easy. Killing another living thing would never be easy. He hated that the evil thoughts had even entered his mind. That's what this man had done to him. Made him someone he hardly recognized. Made him someone who contemplated murder.

The sound of sirens grew close. Dean stirred more, then his eyelids flicked open. "What the..." He tried to push himself up to a seated position, but the shifting snow beneath him and his injury made it difficult.

"Stay where you are," Jonah said. "The sheriff's department is on the way."

Dean groaned, then let himself fall back into the snow.

A sheriff's patrol car pulled up alongside his property. Fortunately, the county had plowed the country road, making it passable. Jonah recognized Deputy Banks the second he climbed out of his vehicle. Jonah waved him down and he immediately felt the tension between his shoulder blades ease. The deputy made his way toward them, taking huge steps. Breathing heavily. His chest heaving. His progress in the deep snow was painfully slow.

As soon as the deputy got within earshot, Dean lumbered to his feet and Jonah took a step back, bracing for the cornered man to lash out.

"He's going to kill me!" Dean hollered, his tone filled with righteous indignation.

Anger throbbed in Jonah's temples. He lifted the gun menacingly. "Shut. Up."

The deputy held out one hand while the other hovered over the butt of his gun in its holster. "Easy there."

Jonah's gaze lifted to the deputy's and his chest tightened when he realized the deputy was talking to him. He shook his head and lowered the gun. "You don't understand."

Dean stepped backward, pointing at his head frantically. Blood trailed down the side of his face. "He's crazy. He tried to kill me, Uncle Eddie!"

Jonah's gaze slid back over to the deputy. "You're family?"

"You have to arrest him," Dean screamed, showing a lot of energy for someone who had been unconscious only moments ago.

The deputy held up his palm to his nephew. "Take it easy, Dean. We'll get to the bottom of this."

"There's nothing to get to the bottom of. He killed Maggie—" Jonah's voice broke over his wife's name "—and this morning, he tried to abduct Daisy."

The deputy's posture sagged a fraction. Resigned. Distraught, maybe. "Turn around." Deputy Banks took a step toward his nephew and teetered forward as his leg sank into the snow. Jonah sucked in a breath, thinking the kid was going to take advantage of the stumble. But Dean simply watched his uncle advance and take the handcuffs from his belt. "Turn around. Kneel down. Put your hands behind your back."

"No, this isn't fair. He hit me. He. Hit. Me," the younger man raged. Spit flew from his mouth as he made short jabbing motions pointing at his head.

"I'm not in the mood, Dean. We'll get this sorted out at the station. Don't make this harder than it already is." The deputy's tone sounded less forceful, more distraught.

Something seemed to register in the young man's face. He fell to his knees and hung his head. Jonah watched as the deputy handcuffed the man and yanked him to his feet.

"Did you know?" Jonah asked, his pulse roaring in his ears. "Did you allow him to use my farm? To get away with murder? Did you look the other way because he was family?"

The deputy shook his head. Jonah had never seen the big, burly police officer look so defeated. "My nephew has always been trouble, but you have to believe me, I had no idea. I always tried to look out for my sister's kid, but there gets to be a point where enough is enough. I'm sorry."

Liddie had rushed Daisy into the house, locked the door, called the sheriff's department and then made sure to get the child warm, dry clothes. Now, Ellen sat on the rocker with her granddaughter in her lap while Andy played on the floor with Snowball, who seemed no worse for wear.

"Where's *Dat*? I want to go play outside, too," Andy said.

Liddie stood off to one side of the window, watching the events unfold. She smiled tightly at Andy, careful not to alarm him. "Be patient."

The little boy released a long-suffering sigh. He grabbed a toy car from the basket and ran it along the floorboards. Her gaze drifted to Daisy, who seemed to have reverted back into herself. It broke Liddie's heart. Ellen ran her hand over the child's head and whispered reassurances. "Everything is going to be fine. *Gott* is *gut*."

"The deputy is here," Liddie said, and released a breath she hadn't realized she'd been holding. She watched the deputy trudge across the snow and she wished she could make out what they were saying.

"Is Jonah on his way in?" Ellen asked, concern lacing her voice.

"Not yet." Liddie didn't take her eyes off the three men. "Okay, Deputy Banks has Dean. He's walking him to the patrol car."

Thank You, Gott.

"The bad man can't hurt us," Daisy whispered, lifting her head. "My *dat* promised."

Liddie crouched down in front of Daisy and Ellen. "You're absolutely right." She smiled at the girl and was rewarded with a faint smile. "You don't have to worry anymore. You're safe."

Daisy nodded and pulled her doll up to her face and hid behind it.

"You were very brave and you protected Snowball." Liddie wanted the little girl to feel empowered. Her chest ached at the thought of Daisy going back to square one emotionally after the shock of today.

A quiet knock sounded at the front door. Snowball wandered over, wagging his tail and sniffing at the door. Liddie planted her hand flat on the door and listened.

"It's Jonah," he called through the door.

She twisted the knob and the dead bolt released. She flung open the door, letting in Jonah on an arctic breeze. She lifted her hands to touch his red face, then self-consciously dropped her arms to her sides, aware of all the eyes on them. "Are you okay?" She looked past him to the deputy plodding through the snow with Dean in handcuffs.

He nodded, a somber expression. He set the shotgun down against the wall and slipped past her. He knelt in front of Daisy. "Are you okay, sweet girl?"

Daisy flung her arms around her *dat* and held tight. Tears burned at the back of Liddie's throat. After a long reunion, Jonah stood and glanced down at the puddle on the hardwood floor under his boots. "I better get out of my wet things." He grabbed the gun and headed into the kitchen.

"I'll make you some tea." Liddie put the kettle on the stove and watched him return the gun to the pantry. He seemed to carry the weight of the world on his shoulders as he put away his winter coat and boots in the mudroom. She reached for mugs in the cabinet when she felt him come up behind her. She slowly turned around and sucked in a breath when she found him standing only inches away, effectively pinning her against the counter.

"I can never thank you enough." His lips twitched as a mix of emotions she couldn't quite pinpoint flickered in his unwavering gaze. Water droplets sat on his beard from the melting snow.

Heat warmed her cheeks. She took a step to the side,

but then stopped and looked up at him. "You never have to thank me for doing what any parent would do. I love Daisy." She drew in a shuddering breath as the emotions of this morning started to catch up to her. "I love Andy. I'd do anything for your children."

He cupped her cheek in his icy hand, ironically leaving a trail of warmth where he gently moved his thumb back and forth. "You were very brave." He searched her eyes and she forced herself not to look away.

She smiled, trying to lighten the moment. "It's easy when you have a shotgun in your hands."

He reached over her head to the open cabinet behind her. She turned a fraction to see what he was doing. He pulled out a box of ammunition. The ammunition he had picked up at the hardware store in town. He shook the box and the bullets rattled. His gaze never wavered from hers. "The gun wasn't loaded."

Her eyes flared wide. "Oh..." She lifted her hand to cover her mouth. "I had no idea."

"Did you think I'd keep a loaded shotgun in the house?"

She shrugged, suddenly feeling a giggle of hysteria bubbling up. She was so cold. Exhausted. Relieved. "I knew I couldn't take him physically...and I had seen the gun in the pantry." She shook her head and blinked slowly. "I barely had time to think."

He tilted his head, seemingly trying to read her thoughts. "You never hesitated when it came time to protect my daughter. I will be forever grateful."

SIXTEEN

Liddie closed her eyes briefly, letting the fresh air wash over her as she sat between the children in the back of the buggy on the way to the Sunday service. Over the last few days, the weather had turned milder—by November's standards in Western New York, anyway—and the snow melted. They had a lot to be grateful for. Although they might never know for sure, Liddie couldn't help but wonder if Deputy Eddie Banks had turned a blind eye to his nephew's criminal acts leading to the delay in his arrest. Or had the uncle actually been complicit in framing Oliver Applegate to protect his sister's son? Yet, another part of her wanted to believe the deputy was completely blindsided by his nephew's behavior.

The kid had kept his relationship to the deputy quiet because he didn't want his trouble-making friends to think he might rat them out. It was a rather amazing secret, especially in a small town. It helped that the sheriff was estranged from his sister, the boy's mother. The deputy claimed to have done his best to keep his nephew in line, while also holding him at arm's length. Seems even law enforcement officers had the occasional black sheep in their family.

The buggy hit a bump, snapping Liddie out of her reverie. She tightened her grip on the glass dish resting on her lap. She leaned to the side, gently nudging Daisy's shoulder with her own. "Snowball's probably napping in his bed right now. Snug as a bug in a rug." She hoped to elicit a smile. Something. Daisy loved that puppy more than anything and had sulked when her father told her she couldn't bring him to Sunday service.

Jonah's daughter stared straight ahead without responding. Liddie supposed it was too much to ask. The recent events had set the poor girl back emotionally and she seemed to withdraw deeper inside herself. But instead of hiding behind the doll her mother had made for her, Liddie had caught the six-year-old chatting quietly to Snowball in an unguarded moment. Liddie would call it progress.

"Looks like we have a bit of a walk," Jonah announced as he parked the buggy at the end of a long row of buggies. "But that's what *Gott* gave us legs for." Ever since Daisy had been rescued and Dean had been arrested, Jonah had a new lightness about him. A side of him Liddie had never seen. It was as if a heavy burden had been lifted. They hadn't discussed their romantic future since that night. She supposed it had been a good thing. The memory of their kiss and what it was supposed to mean could have easily sabotaged their every interaction. Other than his display of gratitude the next morning after she had played a role in saving Daisy, they had gone back to their respective roles as nanny and head of the household. She tried not to overanalyze their relationship and simply counted her blessings, grateful for their new routine. Jonah spent a good chunk of his day in his workshop while Liddie took care of the children. And in the evenings, the five of them gathered for dinner and fellowship.

It was cozy. Comfortable. Something Liddie had been missing at her own house because of her father's ever-present anger. Couldn't he see it was only creating a wedge instead of forging a bond?

The buggy shifted slightly as Jonah hopped off. While he helped the children's grandmother climb down, Liddie scooted off the bench, set the dish on the floorboards, then guided the children to their father's open arms. When he set Andy down, he turned to extend his hand to Liddie. She lifted her gaze and found Ellen smiling at her. The older woman quickly glanced away and took each of the children's hands.

"Come on," Jonah said. Liddie accepted his offer and warmth spread up her arm from where their hands touched. She pulled her hand away as soon as her feet touched the ground. She didn't want to start the tongues wagging in the Amish community.

She laughed to herself. Talk about shutting the barn door after the cows got out, she thought to herself. She was probably going to be the talk of Hickory Lane for the rest of her life even if she settled into domestic bliss from this moment forward. Between her run-in with a gang member from Buffalo to holding a shotgun on Daisy's kidnapper, she had provided plenty of fodder for bored residents of Hickory Lane to chew on.

Making a point of keeping her hands clasped together—where any busybodies could see them—she strolled next to Jonah toward the Lapps' barn while the children walked ahead with Ellen.

"Do you think this was a good idea?" Liddie asked, feeling her palms sweat.

His brow furrowed under his black felt hat. “Coming to service?”

“Coming to service like we’re a family?” They had never done this before. Liddie watched a couple women cutting across the field in front of them, their heads tipped in conversation. “I’m afraid I’m going to be the talk of the town.”

Half his mouth quirked into a grin. “Maybe they’re talking about me.”

Liddie closed her eyes briefly and shook her head. “We make a pair, don’t we?” she whispered, certain that no one would hear them over the steady crunch of their boots on the loose gravel paving the pathway to the barn.

“Do we?” he asked. The hopeful quality of his tone sent her heart fluttering. Why had she decided to bring this up now when they had successfully avoided all talk of romance for days? Before she had a chance to sputter out some silly response, he said, “We have plenty of time to figure things out. We have been blessed with the gift of time. There’s no need to hurry.”

Liddie nodded, not trusting her voice. Up ahead, Andy reached the barn doors and cupped his hands around his mouth to holler to them. “Hurry up!”

Liddie laughed and quickened her pace. “I think we’ve been summoned.”

“We have.” Jonah held out his hand for her to go ahead of him. When they reached the barn, he headed off one way and she, Ellen and the children in another.

Murmured whispers filled the barn and the walls seemed to close in. Were they talking about her? She tugged at her collar. Heat crept up her neck as the eyes of the community seemed to fall on her. Or maybe she was imagining it. Her small group quickly found an empty bench and Daisy scooted in next to her and Andy settled in on the other side of his grandmother. Liddie overheard a few of the women talking about the meal and that's when Liddie remembered the dish she had prepared.

"I forgot to grab the dish from the buggy." She leaned across Daisy to whisper to Ellen. "I should probably get it now so that Mrs. Lapp's not worried if she has enough food."

"It'll keep." Ellen waved her hand in dismissal. "The buggy is cold enough."

Liddie glanced around, disliking the idea that the women might be gossiping about her for not contributing to the communal meal. She suspected her worries were irrational, but she couldn't help herself. "I'm going to grab it all the same. I'll be right back."

A soft smile curved Ellen's lips. "Hurry back."

"Can I go with you?" Daisy whispered and grabbed Liddie's hand.

"Of course. Let's hurry."

Hand in hand, they hustled to the buggy. The last arrivals had already entered the barn-turned-church making her antsy to get back in there. Liddie reached into the buggy and found the dish exactly where she had left it. Daisy tugged on her skirt. "What is it?" She turned around and found her teenage neighbor, Amity, staring at her, a look that made Liddie's blood run cold.

You're just stressed from the past few weeks. It's your neighbor, Amity. You're fine.

Liddie turned around to face the girl, squaring her shoulders. "Hi, Amity," she said, forcing a warmth into her tone that she didn't feel. Her breath grew shallow, sending her into fight-or-flight mode. Liddie glanced around at the empty parking lot, save for the horses and buggies. When the girl didn't answer, Liddie asked, "Are you okay?"

"*Neh*, I'm not. Not at all."

Liddie adjusted her grip on the dish while Daisy hid behind her skirt. "We should get inside. We don't want to be late."

"Can you help me with something?" Amity asked, a sly smile slashing her mouth under cold, dead eyes.

"What is it?" Impatience laced Liddie's tone despite her best efforts at not offending the girl, not wanting to send her over the edge of the perceived cliff she was standing on.

What's going on?

"I need your help over here." Amity moved her head slightly.

Liddie furrowed her brow and an empty fluttering feeling filled her belly. "I can help you later. We're going to be late." She hoisted the dish in her hands a fraction and took a step back, stumbling slightly while careful not to step on Daisy's toes.

"It'll only take a minute." Liddie followed where Amity pointed. The back end of a red van poked out from behind one of the buggies.

Dean Johnson's van? A million questions pinged in her brain. Mounting panic clawed up the back of her throat. "Daisy and I need to get back," Liddie said, forcing an even tone.

Amity lunged at Liddie and grabbed her wrist. The teenager's face contorted in an ugly rage. "You're not going anywhere."

On reflex, Liddie dropped the dish and told Daisy to "Run, run, run!"

Amity took a step toward the child, and her foot slid on the gravel. Unable to stop her, Amity settled for Liddie, digging her bony fingers into her arm and twisting the delicate skin on her wrist. She growled as her eyes snapped wildly, probably realizing she couldn't chase Daisy and hold onto Liddie at the same time. "Get. In. The. Van."

"No." Liddie mustered up more venom in that single word than she had ever felt in her entire life, even more so than when the man abducted her sister. Back then, Liddie didn't fully comprehend the evil that lurked on the edges of a perfectly normal day. Around every corner. She knew better now. And people who threatened to harm children were the worst kind of evil.

"Get in the van!" Amity screeched like a petulant child.

"No," Liddie said, anger bubbling in her chest. She had had enough. She threw all her weight into freeing her wrist, yet couldn't break free.

Amity fumbled behind her back and produced a knife—from the folds of her dress, maybe? Somewhere? It didn't really matter. She had a knife and its tip was pressed to Liddie's wrist. A bead of blood popped up on her white skin. Amity seemed transfixed by it, but Liddie was too fearful to move, not wanting the knife to slice deeper.

"What do you want?" Liddie whispered, this time unable to keep the trembling from her voice.

"For you to pay! You ruined everything!"

Liddie frantically searched over her shoulder and found Daisy peeking out from behind a buggy, her eyes wide with fear. Liddie tried to telegraph a message to the child, "Run, tell your *dat*!"

Jonah greeted the men of his community, many of whom seemed to give a subtle tip of the hat, indicating they had heard of his recent troubles. They'd give him space now, but after the service he'd have to field their questions. He would be surprised if anyone sat next to him, fearful that his bad fortune was contagious. However, the Amish had more trust in *Gott* than some arbitrary fate and his male neighbors filled in on either side of him.

Jonah had just picked up the *Ausbund*, and staring across the barn toward the women, he noticed Liddie and Daisy were missing. He scanned the rows, wondering if perhaps they had sat somewhere else. A solitary voice started singing and the rest of the congregation joined in. He sang along, the words ingrained since childhood, but his eyes kept searching the faces.

Where were they? Icy dread began to pool in the pit of his stomach.

"Dat! Dat!" A terrified cry sounded from the back of the barn. Jonah spun around to find Daisy standing in the doorway screaming for him. The singing trailed away in stages until the last voice went silent.

"Excuse me, excuse me, excuse me." Jonah made his way down the row, bumping into hymnals propped against chests and feet too slow to move. Daisy was still hollering, her frantic cries rising, filling the rafters of the barn. Terror pulsed through his veins.

Jonah reached his daughter and bent down in front of her. "What is it?" His voice scratched in his dry throat.

Daisy grabbed his hand and tugged and tugged and

tugged. "Come quick." His shy girl had been replaced by a confident yet frightened child. Not wanting to make a further scene, Jonah followed her outside, feeling the eyes of the entire community on him.

Daisy led him down the row of buggies. She pointed toward where they had parked. The glass casserole dish and its contents were smashed on the gravel. "What happened? Does Liddie need help?" The weight in his chest began to lift a bit. Was this all it was? A dropped dish?

Daisy shook her head and pointed at a muddy field with tire tracks. "Amity made her go."

"Made Liddie go? What? Where?" The back of his throat ached, yet he kept his voice even. "Daisy, tell me exactly what you saw."

"Amity made her go in the bad man's van. She had a knife."

"The van that you saw at home?"

Daisy nodded, her eyes growing wide. "You said he couldn't get us." His daughter's lower lip quivered. "You said we were safe." The accusation in her tone shattered his heart.

"Nothing's going to happen to you," Jonah said, fighting to keep his voice calm. "Come with me." He ran with Daisy back to the barn. He wove his way through the crowd and his breath hitched when he finally spotted Ellen. She was still sitting on the bench with Andy tucked in next to her. "Stay with your grandmother," Jonah said. Then to Ellen: "Watch her. Don't let either of them out of your sight."

"I won't," Ellen said. "I won't."

Jonah paused long enough to touch her arm gently. "Everything is going to be okay."

Please, Gott, *let everything be okay.*

His neighbors' faces swirled and voices grew distant as he rushed to the door. Abraham Lapp, the homeowner, met him at the barn door as congregants spilled out into the yard. "What's going on?" There was a hard edge to the question, as if he was angry someone dared interrupt the service, especially if that someone was Jonah, a man whose life seemed to invite evil.

"Do you keep a phone on your property? I have an emergency!"

Abraham softened his stance, perhaps reading the fear on Jonah's face. "*Yah*, *yah*, come around to my shop. I have a phone for business."

Matching his urgency, Jonah jogged alongside the man to a small outbuilding where he apparently dealt with *Englischers* while selling produce from his farm. He reached inside and scooped up the phone from the wall and handed it to him.

Jonah dialed 9-1-1 and gave the operator what little information he had. He hung up and turned to Abraham. "Can you make sure my family is safe until I get back? Someone abducted Liddie Miller, my nanny. I'm going to meet a sheriff's deputy down by the road."

Abraham's expression shifted, as if he were going to ask a question, when he seemed to lose the mental war and instead said, "Of course. Your children will be safe here."

"Denki." Jonah gave a quick nod, then sprinted down the lane, the late fall wind hitting his face and whipping his coat open. Once he reached the road, he paced back and forth, back and forth. The bottom of the lane was muddy from the melted snow. The exertion from his run and his growing panic made it difficult to breathe. Finally, a sheriff's patrol car crested the hill with lights

and siren blaring. He let his shoulders sag a fraction when he recognized Deputy Bitsy King through the windshield. Someone he could trust.

Deputy King jumped out of the patrol car. "What's going on, Jonah? Dispatch told me Liddie was abducted."

"*Yah! Yah!* She was dragged into a red van. I think it was Dean Johnson's. Daisy was frantic." He found his gaze drifting up toward the barn. The men in their black hats and coats milled around.

"Go around and get in!" Deputy King said.

Jonah slid into the passenger seat, his panic mounting.

The deputy made a U-turn, churning up gravel. "I spotted a red van turning right onto Younge Street." She shot him quick glances, but kept her eyes mostly on the road. "Johnson's in jail. Who has his van?"

"Amity Beiler. My teenage neighbor." He couldn't wrap his head around the situation. "Amity took Liddie. Daisy said she had a knife." He braced himself as the deputy took the turn on Younge Street without slowing down. "None of this makes sense," he muttered to himself, the fear over losing Liddie stronger than ever.

SEVENTEEN

Liddie held on to the handle of the passenger seat of the van, her hand slicked with sweat. "Why are you doing this, Amity? I don't understand."

"Just shut up!" Amity yelled as her gaze darted around frantically, mostly at the road ahead of them. She held the knife in her right hand against the steering wheel, but she'd randomly extend her arm in Liddie's direction, waving the blade near her face.

"Oh no…" Amity muttered and slowed the vehicle as a patrol car approached from the opposite direction, lights flashing. For the briefest of moments, Liddie considering pulling the door handle and jumping, but before the idea had a chance of catching fire, the patrol car had flown by in the opposite direction and Amity had gunned the engine. Jumping now would only mean certain injury or death, with zero chance of rescue. Amity glanced in the rearview mirror, her breath ragged. She yanked the steering wheel and took a sharp right, slamming Liddie up against the door.

Dear Gott, *protect me.* She had been so uncertain about her faith, her future, but now she wanted more than anything to have both. *Please forgive me for doubt-*

ing. I want to be baptized. Stay here in Hickory Lane. Please forgive me. This was not how things were going to end.

A calm descended over her and she drew in a deep breath.

Amity continued to flick her gaze toward the review mirror. Her shoulders came down from her ears, as if she thought she was in the clear. Liddie watched her abductor's grip on the knife grow more relaxed. Was she fast enough to snag it?

They drove past homes in various states of disrepair. Some set far back from the road. Others built long before the county had paved the winding road. Couches with torn cushions sat on porches. Behind a broken wooden fence a thin horse batted its tail.

Amity glanced once more into the rearview mirror before turning into a muddy lane with tall weeds growing up on either side. The overgrowth whacked the sides of the vehicle as the van bobbled over the ruts. Amity pulled up around the back of a rusted trailer.

"Get out!" Amity demanded.

Liddie pushed open the door and slid out, her feet sinking into the mud. She scanned the area. Could she run and make it to the tree line? To the neighbors? Would anyone even be there? Her mind flashed to that horrible day Jimmy Demmer had taken her and her sister into the empty field not that far from here. She had survived that. She could survive this.

A hollowness expanded in her chest. She prayed Daisy told her father enough information to find her before…

Before what…?

"Amity, why are you doing this?" she tried again.

The teen waved the knife around, making Liddie calculate if she could outrun her.

"Go! Go! Go!" an internal voice screamed. Adrenaline surged and she spun on her heel. The mud made it like a skating rink and she went down hard. She yelped her frustration. Amity was on her, pressing the knife casually against her neck. One false move and her life would be over. No more worries about her future. She fought the tears that burned the back of her eyes. Why had she been so indecisive? Easy to do when she had a choice.

A future.

Liddie asked in an even voice, "What do you want from me?" Did she have a crush on Jonah? Liddie had long suspected the young woman wanted her out of the picture, but she had no idea of the lengths she'd go.

"Stand up," Amity commanded Liddie. Slowly, she stood and gingerly touched her coat with mud-caked hands. Amity positioned herself behind her and pushed. "Get moving." Liddie moved forward, her boots slipping in the mud until they reached a wooden back porch with spongey floorboards. "Open the door." Liddie did as she was instructed. The metal hinges groaned. "Go in!" Apparently, the girl would only speak in short, declarative statements.

Liddie entered the small space that served as a kitchen. A pan of something burnt rested on one of the burners, dirty dishes sat in the sink, something small and fast skittered across the counter. Goose bumps blanketed Liddie's arms. She slowly turned around, but nothing prepared her for what she saw: the wild-eyed look of her neighbor clawing at her hair, yanking it out of her tight bun.

"Amity, everything will be okay," Liddie said in the best soothing tone she could muster. "Tell me what's going on."

"You. Ruined. Everything." Spittle flung from the teenager's mouth. "Everything!" she screamed, her face contorting in rage.

Liddie racked her brain for something to say. To somehow calm this girl down. "Who lives here?" She measured her words, trying to act casual. The old trailer seemed closed up and smelled stale.

"You don't understand any of this, do you? It's all about you." Amity jabbed the knife into her side, stopping short of cutting her. "You couldn't leave it be."

Liddie narrowed her gaze, taking a step back, creating a fraction of space between her ribs and the weapon. The air was charged with a frantic energy that made it hard for Liddie to think straight. She held her questions, giving Amity room to talk.

"He didn't want to raise our family here."

A blanket of pinpricks smothered Liddie as realization finally wormed its way into her consciousness. The red van.

"He only needed one more growing season to have enough money to take us away from here and you ruined it all. We were going to get our own house away from all the dumb rules. Away from everyone who would have shunned me for not being a good girl."

"Amity, you need to be reasonable."

Amity held up her hand. "I'm done being reasonable." She leaned back against a plaid couch that separated a seating area from the tight quarters of the kitchen. She set the knife down on the cushion behind her. Liddie quickly lifted her gaze away from it so that she wouldn't realize her potential mistake. A faraway look descended into Amity's eyes. "Jonah was too busy with work. He never paid attention. The path was clear until you came on the scene. Your daily walks." Her eyes narrowed. "And Daisy." Amity shook her head, as if working it all out. "No one would have believed her if you hadn't kept pushing it. She's a stupid kid. No one listens to kids."

"Some people do."

An ugly expression crumpled Amity's face. "That's where you made a mistake."

"It's over, Amity. Dean's in jail."

"And I'm stuck in this stupid town."

Liddie had to keep Amity talking. Had to find a way out. "I didn't know you and Dean were dating."

Amity's eyes flared wide, then narrowed into dangerous slits. "We were going to get married as soon as he had enough money. I found the land for him to grow the marijuana. I knew Jonah would never, ever find it. He had no interest in farming."

"And Maggie." Tears burned the back of Liddie's eyes at the mention of the poor woman who had lost her life. Who would never see her children grow up. But Liddie was still here. She could see these things. Do these things. She had a future if only she could escape.

"I don't know why Maggie went back there. To the greenhouse." Amity's nose scrunched up at the mention of it and she scrubbed away at her scalp again, as if lice had sprung from the old cushions and infested her hair. Her bun hung loose and strands sprang out of the hairpins in all directions. "No one had been in the greenhouse for years. Maggie's parents only farmed a fraction of the land. It was a perfect choice."

Amity shook her head slowly, red suddenly rimming her eyes. "He didn't want to hurt her, but she would have ruined everything. His friend Oliver was there that day so spaced out—on some crazy drug, not marijuana—that it was easy to convince him he had done something wrong. You know?" she added casually. "They grew and sold marijuana, but they were into scarier drugs. I think they fried Oliver's brain. It didn't take much to convince him and the sheriff's department that he did it."

"Did Deputy Banks know what his nephew was doing?" Liddie whispered through a throat tight with emotion.

Amity made a horrified sound with her lips. "No way. That man is clueless. He believed each and every one of Dean's lies. I suppose families want to believe what they want to believe." Amity thumped Liddie in the chest with a bony index finger forcing her to take a stumbling step backward. She caught herself on the counter. "You were the only person left in our way."

"Oh, Amity. You have to stop this now." She swallowed, feeling the walls growing close. "No one else has to get hurt." She felt behind her and picked up a glass jar and calculated the risk of smashing it over her captor's head.

Amity's eyes grew dark. "I'm already hurt. There's no going back." She leaned over and snatched the knife and hoisted it menacingly. Liddie feared if she moved even an inch, her unstable neighbor would plunge the blade into her heart.

The engine of the patrol car revved as Deputy King floored it. "I'm not going to turn on the siren. We don't want to spook her."

"If we can find her." Jonah searched the properties on Younge Street. There were so many places to hide a van. "They could be miles away by now." He felt sick to his stomach. How had he not realized how troubled his neighbor was?

"I don't think so." Deputy King slowed and pulled over to the side of the road and put the gear into Park. She leaned forward and pointed through the windshield. "Look there."

Jonah squinted. The back end of a van stuck out from behind a trailer deep among the trees. His heart raced. "Is that it?"

"I can't be sure, but I think so." The deputy gave her location to dispatch and asked for backup. "I talked to Eddie at length after Dean was arrested. He told me his nephew had a piece of land he was hoping to build a house on. He gave me the address. I was out here the other day, checking it out. I think he was trying to rationalize why he was intent on growing marijuana at all costs."

"Including killing Maggie," Jonah said flatly. "Did the deputy mention Dean's ties to my neighbor?"

"No, he didn't mention anyone else."

"Okay." Jonah patted his thighs nervously and pushed his felt hat up farther on his head. "Guess we won't find out if that's them unless we go—"

"Whoa, whoa…" Deputy King said. "We have to wait for backup."

"The Amish might not be a fan of law enforcement, but we both know that's going to take more time than we have." Without waiting for a response, Jonah pushed open the door and climbed out and ducked his head back into the opening. "I'm going to check out that van."

The deputy's eyes widened as she reached for her door release. "You need to wait."

Jonah didn't wait.

Behind him, he heard the thwack of the overgrown brush as the deputy jogged up behind him. "Wait!"

Jonah spun around. "I'm not going to wait. Either come with me or wait for backup. Your choice. I'm not going to lose someone I love again." He was too jacked up on adrenaline to analyze what he had just said. But he knew deep in his heart that he had fallen hard for his children's nanny.

The deputy muttered something under her breath as she unholstered her gun and slipped in front of him. "Stay behind me."

When they reached the van, Jonah noticed the markings on it. It was definitely Dean's. His mouth went dry as he turned to look at the window of the run-down trailer, cloudy from dirt.

A crash sounded from the far side of the trailer. "I'm going to check that out," the deputy whispered. "Stay here behind the van." She paused for a fraction, narrowing her gaze. "Stay low."

Jonah hunkered down on the side of the van as the deputy crouched low and ran around to the front of the trailer. He wasn't going to stay here and wait. He had to take action. With his back close to the van, he moved toward the trailer. He peered around. The back door swung freely in the breeze.

Heart beating wildly in his chest, he ran to the back and stepped up on the old porch. He stood off to one side, and reached over and flung the door all the way open. He peeked around and his stomach bottomed out. Amity held a knife to a cornered Liddie. Jonah exploded inside. The powerful smell of decay nearly overpowered him.

"Help me!" Liddie hollered.

Jonah grabbed Amity's wrist and yanked the knife away from her. "Enough!"

A scream ripped from the teenager's throat as she lifted her fist. Before he had a chance to do anything, Liddie planted both hand on the girl's shoulders and shoved her. Amity landed with a crash in the tight space between the bench seat and the cabinets.

"Everything's ruined!" she muttered, all the fight having drained from her. "Everything."

Deputy King arrived and did a double take. "Everyone okay?" Without waiting for an answer, she scooted past them and yanked Amity to her feet. "What's that red stuff all over the windows? Is someone bleeding?"

"No. I threw a jelly jar but I missed my target."

"Lucky for your target." The deputy nudged Amity forward. "Let's get you out of here."

Jonah and Liddie followed the deputy outside. As the deputy stuffed Amity into the back of the patrol car, he turned to Liddie. "Are you okay?"

"I am now."

Jonah touched her face gently and whispered, "Are we done with all of this?"

A slow smile brightened her face. "*Yah*, I'm definitely done with all of this."

With the adrenaline ebbing from Liddie's system, a quiet trembling coursed through her and she couldn't stop shaking. "We need to get the children," Jonah whispered, dropping his hand from her face. She immediately missed his calming touch. He ushered her to the patrol car.

Deputy King stood outside the open car door. "I called off backup, but I did request a ride for you two." She tipped her head toward the passenger in her back seat. Amity had her eyes closed and her head tilted back. It looked like she had exhausted herself. "They'll be here in minutes. You both okay?"

"*Yah*, thank you," Liddie said. She crossed her arms tightly across her midsection and tried to stem the quiet quaking that threatened to consume her now that the danger had passed. She didn't know how much more of this she could take. She didn't know how she had stopped Amity from stabbing her. She swallowed hard, trying not to imagine how differently this could have ended.

Thank Gott *for protecting me.*

"After I take Amity in, I'll come by your house so I can get your statement." The deputy flipped up her collar against the breeze. "Unless you changed your mind about the hospital."

"I don't need the hospital. I'm fine." *Gott* had been watching over her, that's for sure. And then Jonah showed up. She thought, at first, that she had willed him into appearing.

"Are you sure?" The concern in his voice warmed her heart.

"I promise you, I'm fine."

"You know how to take care of yourself."

She could only imagine the scene Jonah encountered when he burst into the trailer.

"Don't worry. We'll make sure Amity gets proper care," the deputy interrupted. "I grew up Amish and it wasn't that long ago that I was a teenager. I have to wonder what's gotten into some of these youth. I certainly don't look forward to paying her family a visit. They'll be devastated."

"They're *gut* people," Jonah said, frowning. "I can't imagine what it would be like to learn Daisy or Andy had done..." He let his voice trail off.

"Your children would never," Liddie reassured him. Yet Daisy had witnessed so much violence in her short life. An ache twisted Liddie's gut at the mere thought of it, convincing her more than ever that she wanted to be a part of Daisy's healing process. She met Jonah's warm gaze. She prayed their blossoming romance didn't fizzle, leaving Daisy as collateral damage. Maybe it wasn't a risk worth taking. Maybe she should stop this courtship in its tracks, securing her nanny position instead. Making sure she was there for Daisy.

But even that couldn't last forever.

"Are you sure you're okay?" Jonah asked, his warm voice a balm to her frazzled nerves. "You look lost."

Liddie shook her head and smiled. "I'm cold."

The deputy extended her hand. "There's your ride. The sheriff's department will pay the fare, don't worry."

Jonah opened the back door and Liddie climbed into the back seat. Thankfully, the heat pumped from the vents. She held up her hands to warm them. Feeling Jonah's steady gaze, she turned and raised her eyebrows expectantly. A flutter of attraction warmed her heart.

"I'm so glad you're okay." He gently touched her hand and left it there.

"Me, too."

When they reached his farm, the children and Ellen were waiting for them.

Ellen met them outside on the porch. "Mr. Lapp brought us home. We wanted to be here when you arrived. Poor Daisy."

"Where is she?" Liddie asked.

"In the house with Snowball."

Liddie gave Jonah a quick glance before rushing into the house. She sensed Jonah behind her, but kept her focus on his daughter. She crouched down in front of Daisy as she petted her constant companion. "How's Snowball?"

Daisy looked up through her long eyelashes. *"Gut."*

Liddie settled in cross-legged on the floor. "You did a very brave thing at the Lapps' farm."

Daisy straightened. "Why was Amity mad at you?"

"She got involved with some bad people and she was afraid I was going to tell on her."

Daisy pressed her lips into a thin line. "Did you tell on her?"

"I didn't know she had done anything wrong. But now she's in jail and she can't hurt me. Or you. Or anyone. Not anymore."

Daisy's eyes grew wide. "She can't hurt anyone?"

Something in the seriousness of Daisy's questions sent Liddie's heart racing. "Did Amity hurt you?" Her mind went back to the day they found Daisy locked in the barn. Dean had already confessed, but had Amity been involved, too?

The little girl lifted one shoulder. Jonah knelt down next to them. "I promise you no one is going to hurt you or your brother." He placed a hand on Liddie's shoulder. "Or Liddie."

Daisy nodded, more confident this time. "Or Snowball?"

Jonah reached out to pet the dog and his hand collided with Liddie's. "No one that I care about."

"*Gut*, because she told me I could have Snowball as long as I never told anyone that she played a trick on me."

"What trick?" Liddie found herself holding her breath, waiting for the answer.

"She locked me in the barn after that bad man grabbed me. She said if I told, she'd take back Snowball." Daisy started to cry. "And hurt him."

"That will never happen. I promise," Liddie said around a lump of emotion in her throat.

"Come sit with me," Ellen said, drawing in her granddaughter. "We'll cuddle by the fire."

"Thank you," Jonah said.

Liddie pushed to her feet and caught Jonah's attention. She asked him to join her on the front porch so they could talk in private.

"I can't believe Amity was involved in all this." His anger charged the air.

Liddie reached out and boldly brushed the back of his hand. "Amity's going to get the punishment she deserves, but that's not what I want to talk about."

When she dropped her hand, he reclaimed it and warmth spread up her arm from his touch. She dipped her head, suddenly feeling shy. He tilted his head. "What's on your mind?" The question felt intimate as he stood inches from her, the warmth of his body noticeable with the surrounding cool fall air.

"I don't ever want to let your children down," she whispered, the words strangled with emotion.

"You'd never let my children down." He gently squeezed her hand. "You've been the best thing that has happened to them." He seemed to cut himself off short, but she suspected he was going to say, "and me," which made what she had to say so much harder.

She reclaimed her hand and crossed her arms tightly over her chest. "If whatever this is…" she jerked her chin in his direction "…if whatever this is fizzles out, you'll want me to leave and I don't know if I can do that to the children, especially Daisy." Every thought that had been swirling around in her head didn't sound any more rational when she spoke them out loud.

He took a small step back and lifted his hand to gently brush her cheek with the back of his knuckles. "What are you saying?" His words were weighted with expectation.

"Perhaps I should just be their nanny." There was no danger in being their nanny, except that she'd have to see Jonah every day and wonder about what could have been. And what if he met someone else? In a way, she felt trapped in an impossible situation. She wanted to protect her heart. The children's hearts. But there didn't seem to be a clear path to avoiding hurt. And she had had enough of that in her young life.

"Is that what you want?" The pain she had been struggling to avoid was evident in his voice.

"I want to be there for the children and I'm afraid our relationship could jeopardize that."

He shook his head and a tremble of regret coursed through her. "That won't work for me."

Her heart started to race. "But…"

Jonah closed the distance between them. "That won't work because I've fallen for you. If you need more time to figure things out, I'm okay with that. But I want to be more than the father of the children you watch. I want to be your future."

Liddie swallowed hard. "I want that, too. But I'm afraid. I don't want to get hurt."

"I'll keep you safe." Jonah drew her into his arms and held her close. "You don't need to be afraid anymore." He planted a kiss on her forehead and she breathed in his clean scent. The fresh air. Soaking in this moment.

Jonah continued, "As Daisy would say, 'The bad guys are in jail.'" He angled his face to study hers. "If you're going to avoid getting close to anyone because you're afraid, well—" he smiled "—you'll miss out on the best parts of life. I don't know about you, but I think some people are worth taking that risk for."

Liddie rested her cheek on his chest and closed her eyes. She felt safe. She felt loved.

"Sometimes it takes a little faith." His deep voice rumbled through her. *Faith.*

Liddie lifted her face to search his expression. Everything she ever wanted was reflected in his eyes. He hiked an eyebrow as if to say, "What do you think?" She got up on her tiptoes and planted a kiss on his lips.

Gott had brought her to this farm. To these children. To this man. Exactly where she was meant to be. It took faith, she realized.

"You're right. I'm willing to take a leap."

Jonah slid his hands up to her cheeks and tipped his forehead against hers. "Let's just keep both feet on the ground for a bit."

EIGHTEEN

Ten months later...

Jonah pulled back on the reins, slowing the workhorses in the field where he had been binding corn. He held up his hand to block the late afternoon sun and scanned his property. A sense of pride swelled in his chest. His beautiful home. The barn. The space that had once been a greenhouse had been replaced by a wildflower garden in memory of his first wife and tended to by Liddie and the children. It had been Liddie's idea. His heart swelled.

On the country road, sunlight reflected off a vehicle as it slowed. He watched as it turned onto his property. Jonah hollered over his shoulder, "Looks like our company is here!"

Elijah and Caleb, Liddie's younger brothers, secured the bound cornstalks and jumped off the wagon whooping and hollering. With the winding down of summer, Jonah was approaching the end of his first growing season, the first on this land since his former in-laws had farmed it. Liddie's younger brothers came over when they could, splitting their time between both farms.

Jonah knew it wasn't sustainable, but it would do for now. He double-checked the load of bound cornstalks and hopped back up front and grabbed the reins. He flicked his wrists and the horses lurched forward toward the barn.

Tomorrow was another day.

By the time Jonah made sure the horses were fed and settled, Liddie had already invited her sister and family inside. Their shiny vehicle looked out of place on the tranquil Amish farm.

Finally tranquil. It had taken a long time, but things had finally fallen into place.

After he cleaned up, he found Daisy and Andy in the sitting room fawning over their new cousin, who was cooing and smiling in his mother's lap. He was struck by how much Liddie looked like her older sister Bridget, if the *kapp* and bun were replaced with a fancy haircut and stylish clothes.

"You made it," Jonah said, smiling a bit too brightly, eager to make a good first impression on Liddie's sister and brother-in-law. What would they think of him? A simple Amish farmer.

Zach Bryant, the DEA agent, stood and extended his hand with a broad smile. "It's great to finally meet you."

"We are so glad you came!" Liddie's hesitant smile reflected some of his nerves. She had been up before dawn helping Ellen clean the house top to bottom, as if she had something to prove. "You have to meet Caitlin. Isn't she the most beautiful baby?" Liddie was practically beaming. She tipped her head and smiled at her brothers. "You boys have another niece."

Elijah and Caleb wandered over to inspect their sister's baby. Caleb reached out and Bridget smiled. "You might want to wash up from the fields first."

"I see someone still thinks she's the boss," Elijah said in a playful tone and without missing a beat, he gently slugged his brother in the shoulder. "Let's wash up. I hope dinner's almost ready. I'm starving."

"After you wash up, you can help drag the picnic table into the shade," Ellen hollered from where she was doing last-minute dinner preparations. "The baby doesn't need to have the sun beating down on her beautiful skin."

Jonah watched his borrowed field hands hustle off to the utility sink to do as they were told, then he turned back to his company. "Must have been a long drive." He rubbed his hands together, trying to imagine a 400-mile trip in one day. The daily van trips back and forth to Buffalo had grown old and once he decided to work on the farm, he didn't miss the commute or the construction work at all. He still did his woodworking when the mood struck, but now with Liddie, he enjoyed spending his free time with her and the children.

"Wasn't too bad. The baby slept for a good chunk of it," Zach said.

"We'll pay for that tonight." Bridget planted a kiss on the baby's head and as if on cue, the baby fussed.

Daisy disappeared and came back a few moments later and placed her favorite doll on the baby's lap. "Here, baby, don't cry."

"What a pretty doll," Bridget said, gently adjusting the fabric of its dress. The baby settled in and her eyes grew heavy. "Oh, looks like your doll did the trick." She offered the doll back to Daisy. "Thank you for sharing."

Daisy shook her head. "I'd like Caitlin to have it."

Jonah met Liddie's gaze and held. She covered her mouth with her hand, and the simple gold band reflected the late afternoon sun beaming in through the window. Something deep in his heart hitched.

"Denki," Bridget said. "We'll make sure we bring your doll every time we visit."

The little children asked to go outside with the older boys to set up the table for dinner and the baby settled in for a nap.

"Here, let me put the baby down." Zach scooped up the baby, tucking the doll in next to her. "You said there was a bassinette in our room?"

"*Yah*, it's all set up in the bedroom at the top of the stairs," Liddie said.

"Well, I'll let you two catch up," Jonah said.

"No, hold on a minute," Bridget said. "I'd like to talk a bit with the man who finally was able to get my sister to settle down."

Jonah's gaze drifted to Liddie, whose cheeks brightened. "Jonah made the choice easy. I was baptized and we married as soon as we could."

"The bishop probably didn't want you to wait until autumn." Bridget laughed. Most Amish weddings occurred after the fall harvest. "In case you changed your mind."

"Bridget, stop teasing," Liddie said playfully, then grew serious. "I'd never change my mind."

Jonah smiled and reached out to gently squeeze his wife's hand. "I'll go check on the children." He slipped out of the room, forever grateful that happiness once again filled his home.

Sitting in the rocking chair next to Bridget, Liddie clasped her sister's hand and practically squealed. "I'm so happy you were able to come, especially with the baby."

"I'm happy to be here, too. I can't wait for *Mem* and *Dat* to meet her."

"Have you talked to *Dat*?" Liddie asked, finding herself holding her breath as she waited for the answer.

"I did. Briefly." Bridget smiled, but it didn't reach her eyes. "He's proud of you. I could hear it in his voice."

"We've had to mend a lot of fences over the past year," Liddie said. "Our relationship's not perfect, but it's much better than it had been. It helped that I married a nice Amish man."

Bridget released a quiet breath through her nose, and Liddie realized she had put her foot in her mouth. "I mean..."

"No, no, it's fine. I'm surprised Father agreed to a visit from me. I'm not exactly the perfect Amish daughter."

"You've built a wonderful live with Zachary, and now the baby." Liddie carefully chose her words. "It has to be hard for Amish parents. They want the best for their children, yet they have the added pressure of raising their children to remain among the Amish." She frowned. "I'm sure I'll feel the same way when Daisy and Andy get older."

"Ah, thankfully you won't have to face that for a long time." Her sister's voice held a nostalgic note.

"If your beautiful baby can't soften up *Dat* I don't know what will," Liddie said, longing to encourage her sister. A beautiful *Englisch* baby wasn't the way to reconcile with their strict Amish father, but they also knew their father's love for their mother wouldn't allow him to forbid a visit. What grandparent didn't want to meet their grandchild?

"I have faith that you're right," Bridget said. "And I'm glad you and Jonah will be coming with us."

"Oh," Liddie said, "I hope you don't mind that the children's aunt and their cousins will be coming for a visit while you're here."

"Maggie's sister?" Hearing Jonah's deceased wife's name on her sister's lips sounded odd.

Liddie nodded. "Turns out our family isn't the only one that needed to mend fences. Ruthann and Jonah had a bit of a falling out." She lowered her voice so as not to be overheard. "She had wanted this farm for her family."

"Really?"

Heat flooded Liddie's face and she waved her hand in dismissal. "I shouldn't gossip. Their differences seem to be in the past. Ruthann and Jonah want to make sure their children grow up knowing their cousins."

"That's wonderful," Bridget said. "I hope Caitlin stays close with hers."

"Of course." Liddie's voice cracked with emotion.

"Jonah seems really nice," Bridget said, seemingly eager to change the subject.

"Who would have thought I'd be married so soon?" Liddie had enjoyed writing long detailed letters to her sister. The first explained the excitement on the farm and how she couldn't believe evil had found her again. Her big sister had written back, joking that Liddie must be a magnet for the bad guys.

Subsequent letters told of her blossoming romance and her surprisingly quick baptism and her marriage to Jonah. They were able to marry in January—an off month for Amish weddings—in a small ceremony.

Even though Ellen still lived with them, it felt like less tongues would wag if they were married after their growing affection became obvious. More than one person had approached their little family after a church service or two, trying to ruminate about their relationship. In private, Jonah and Liddie laughed, speculating the bishop wanted to hurry up and have her join the church before they lost her. There were probably whispers of truth to that.

"Sometimes things just work out the way they're meant to," Bridget said, tracing one of the grains in the wood on the arm of the rocker. "I hope maybe some time you and Jonah and the children can come visit us in Virginia." Her smile quickly faded and Liddie was eager to make her feel better.

"Perhaps we could make the trip to deliver a rocking chair for you and the baby. Jonah makes such beautiful pieces."

"Sounds wonderful." Bridget leaned forward, and the chair dipped as she slid up to the edge. "Maybe you could time it with the baby's baptism." Her big sister waved her hand, seemingly self-conscious. "I mean, maybe you could celebrate with us at the house afterward if you're too uncomfortable to come into the church. I know it's not how the Amish do it, and all."

"I'll talk to Jonah, but I'm sure he'd love to go on an adventure. We'd have to time it with work here on the farm."

"Of course." Bridget leaned back in the chair and seemed to settle in.

"I'm happy you found a church, even if it's not Amish. I didn't realize until I had fully come back to my faith how much I was struggling without it."

Bridget reached out and squeezed her sister's hand. "You're so right."

"So, is parenting everything you thought it would be?" Liddie asked, eager to learn more about her sister's life in Virginia. "You must be a pro with Caitlin after working as a nurse with those precious high-risk babies."

"Nothing fully prepares you for taking care of your own baby, but yeah, I do think caring for the sickest babies makes you learn to take things in stride, especially when you're blessed with a healthy baby." Her sister's tone oozed with love.

"Will you go back to work at the hospital?" Liddie had a hard time imagining handing over that sweet little baby for strangers to watch. "It's too bad we don't live closer. I'd love to watch Caitlin. So would Daisy and Andy."

"I'll take a year off, for sure. And then we'll see where life takes me."

Voices sounded through the open window. Liddie dipped her head to look out. "The picnic table is all set. Why don't you go outside? I'll be there in a few minutes. I want to help Ellen."

A quick frown flashed on her sister's face. "I hope you're not going to treat me like a guest in my own sister's home."

Liddie jerked her head back a fraction and smiled. "Of course not, I just thought you'd need a break after your long drive."

The two women wandered into the kitchen and Bridget picked up a dish to pass. "I've been sitting for hours. Carrying a few dishes outside is hardly taxing."

Liddie caught Ellen's gaze. The woman who had

once upon a time judged the Outsider—the nanny—who had invaded her daughter's home gave the two women a warm smile. "Many hands make light work." She grabbed a dish herself and turned toward the door. "Let's hurry up. The men are probably hungry."

Later that night, Liddie made sure all her houseguests had everything they needed. She climbed the stairs and was surprised to find Bridget in PJ bottoms and a T-shirt pacing the floor outside of the bedroom with sweet baby Caitlin fussing in her arms. A soft glow of a lantern flickered in the landing.

Bridget smiled at her approaching sister. "I think we have a night owl on our hands." She pivoted and walked the other way and then returned. "She's been fed, changed, and she's still like, 'Hi, Mommy, I want to be held.'"

Liddie held out her arms. "Let me take her so you can sleep."

Bridget's eyes flared wide with a mixture of disbelief and gratitude. "Are you sure? Weren't you headed off to bed yourself?"

"Oh, come to Aunt Liddie, sweet little one." She gently took the baby into her arms and drew her close, running her hand in a soft circular motion on her back, drinking in the smell and feel of her. "I'd happily trade some sleep to spend time with my niece."

Bridget dragged a hand through her shoulder-length hair. It still struck Liddie as out of place after growing up with a sister whose hair grew down past her waist. "If you're sure," she said around a yawn.

"I'm sure. Just leave your bedroom door ajar and

I'll sneak in and put her in the bassinette after I get her to sleep."

Bridget leaned in and kissed the baby on the top of her head, then brushed a kiss on Liddie's cheek. "You're the best."

Liddie smiled, then went downstairs. She settled into the rocking chair and cooed at the baby, telling her how lucky she was to have such a wonderful mommy and how one day when she was older, her auntie would share stories about what it was like growing up on a farm.

It didn't take long for the baby to drift off, her chubby cheek smooshed against Liddie's chest. Liddie leaned back and closed her eyes, enjoying the subtle back and forth of the rocking chair and the sweet scent of her niece's head.

Liddie had just dozed off when she felt Jonah's beard brush her forehead. "You look content," he said, his voice low and deep.

"Bridget had trouble getting the baby to sleep," Liddie whispered, angling her head to catch a glimpse of the baby's face in the soft flickering light. Her tiny chest rose and fell.

"Looks like you did just fine." Jonah sat down in the rocking chair next to hers, his gaze fixed on hers.

"Thank you for welcoming my family." She adjusted the edges of the soft pink blanket wrapped around the baby. "I know some people will gossip about us having *Englisch* visitors in our home."

"I'd rather they speculate about an innocent family visit than all the things that had gotten their tongues wagging previously."

"So true." Both she and Jonah had been through so much over the past few years. To even worry if someone judged them for hosting her *Englisch* sister, brother-in-law and baby seemed silly.

"Daisy and Andy were so happy to meet their cousin." There was a dreamy quality to his voice.

"Daisy will make a wonderful little mother's helper someday," Liddie said, wondering if *Gott* was going to bless them with a child sooner rather than later. The past few mornings, her stomach felt queasy, but she had written it off to nerves ahead of her sister's visit. She hadn't said anything to Jonah yet because she didn't want to disappoint him if it wasn't true.

"*Yah*, all big sisters tend to be little helpers in large Amish families."

"Speaking of big Amish families, Mrs. Beiler wandered over earlier today when you were working in the field." Liddie hated to spoil such a peaceful moment with news from their days of hardship, but the troubled Amish neighbor had a tendency to pop into her mind now and again. Jonah and Liddie had decided not to pursue charges against Amity for her part in being a lookout for her drug dealer boyfriend and his friends. Instead, the family had decided to send her away to a relative's home in Ohio. "It seems Amity is getting married in a couple of weeks."

Jonah raised a skeptical eyebrow.

"Apparently to a nice Amish boy. The family feels she's changed."

"I hope she has." His simple statement still held a hint of a hard edge. Jonah had proclaimed forgiveness, but she knew he still struggled. It was natural. She supposed it helped that Dean was in jail and was expected to spend the rest of his life there.

"Mrs. Beiler asked us to keep an eye on the property. They'll be out of town that weekend."

"Seems ironic, right? For us to keep an eye on their farm when their daughter…" He scrubbed a hand over his face. "*Gott* knows I'm trying to forgive."

"You're doing just fine."

Jonah must have noticed Liddie's subtle squirm as she adjusted her tingling arm under the baby. "Here, let me hold her," he said.

"Really?" Liddie didn't hide her disbelief. When she first moved in to be the children's nanny, Jonah rarely interacted with them. That slowly changed over the course of months, but she had often wondered how he would be with a baby. Most men she knew deferred all childrearing to the mother, especially when it came to little ones.

"*Yah*, I'm sure. I've held a baby before." Jonah stood and bent over, carefully taking the baby from her. Caitlin looked so tiny in his large hands and Liddie's heart softened. A warmth spread through her veins. She didn't think it was possible to love this man any more than she already did. He settled into the rocker and adjusted the blanket away from the baby's face. "Hello, little one."

Liddie found herself staring at her husband. Wondering why *Gott* had seen to bless her with such a wonderful life when not that long ago she struggled to find her place in this world. Turned out it was in Hickory Lane. As the wife of Jonah Troyer.

He lifted his face and smiled. "It will be nice when we have a little one of our own."

Liddie's heart began to race. Did he suspect something? The butterflies in her belly made her want to blurt out her news. She reached out and touched his strong hand supporting the baby's head. "I think we may be blessed, sooner rather than later."

A smile unlike one she had ever seen brightened her husband's face. "Are you?"

"I'm not sure, but I think..." She shrugged and gingerly placed her other hand on her abdomen. "I hope."

Jonah adjusted the baby in his arms and reached over to cover Liddie's hand with his. "I'm confident *Gott* will bless us with whatever is *gut* for our family. He has already blessed me beyond measure."

Liddie blinked and felt a tear escape down her cheek.

Jonah pulled back his hand and a flash of concern swept across his handsome face. "What is it? Are you not feeling well?"

A slow smile pulled on her lips. "I don't think I've ever been happier."

"Me, neither."

"Perhaps we should get the little one into the bassinette before she wakes up again."

Jonah nodded and passed her the baby. He followed her up the stairs with a protective hand on the small of her back. A warm, cozy feeling swirled around her and she had an odd sense. As if time had passed. They were retiring for the night, ready to put their child to bed. Not her niece.

It felt so real.

If anyone had told her she'd be where she was now almost two years ago after she had made terrible choices, she wouldn't have believed them. Her heart and mind had been weighted down by uncertainty. Doubt. But, now, outside her sister's bedroom door, ready to put her infant niece to bed, she had an overwhelming sense that her happiness wouldn't be fleeting.

A blessed future. One with her husband, Daisy, Andy and any babies *Gott* saw fit to bless them with. Yes, she truly did believe.

She had faith.

* * * * *

Look for Bridget's story, Seeking Amish Shelter, *available now wherever Love Inspired Suspense books are sold!*

Dear Reader,

Thank you for reading *Amish Country Cover-Up*, my second book set in Hickory Lane, a fictional town in Western New York. I hope you had as much fun following the story of Bridget's younger sister Liddie, who got in trouble during *Rumspringa* in the first book in the series, *Seeking Amish Shelter.* As a result, Liddie was struggling to find her way, which led her to take a job as a nanny for a recent Amish widower. And, of course, where Liddie goes, "bad stuff" follows. (Sorry, I don't want to give away the plot in case you're reading this letter first!) Even though there is an overlap of characters, and both books are set in Hickory Lane, each story can be read as a standalone.

Writing *Amish Country Cover-Up* was a wonderful escape during a very trying time in the world when my entire family was quarantined in my home during the height of the pandemic. It reinforced the notion that books are a wonderful form of escape. Readers can follow the twists and turns of the characters' lives knowing, especially in the Love Inspired Suspense line, that the heroine will find love and the bad guys will get their comeuppance. There is a certainty that we often can't find in the real world. So, I hope you enjoyed this little break from the world.

Meanwhile, I'll be plotting more mayhem for my next book.

I love to hear from my readers via email at Alison@AlisonStone.com.

Be well.
Live, Love, Laugh,
Alison Stone

Movement from the edge of the porch caught her attention. “Hey, who’s there?”

The slow-moving sun only revealed the silhouette of a man simply standing there. Not moving. Just watching. Unease crawled through her. “Hey, is this your baby?”

Still, he stayed silent. He looked back over his shoulder one more time, then seemed to make up his mind about something. Her nerves jangled and alarm shuddered through her. He took a step toward her and Isabelle spun. Holding the infant in the crook of her left arm, she twisted the knob with her right hand and pushed the door open just wide enough for her to slip through. She shut the door and locked it.

He moved as though to leave, then turned back, dark eyes on hers. He came toward the glass door, reaching for the knob. Isabelle whirled and raced to her bedroom to snatch her phone from the nightstand. She dialed 911 and hurried back to the den area to see the dark-clad figure pacing in front of her door. Quick as lightning, he spun and slammed a fist on the wooden part of the door. The noise jarred the infant, who let out a wail.

“911. What’s your emergency?”

“Someone’s trying to get in my house.”

LISEXP0621

When someone tries to take an infant from her ranch, foster mother Isabelle Trent gets caught in the would-be abductor's deadly sights. With her ranch hand, Brian "Mac" McGee, at her side, they will do anything to protect the baby.

Read on for a sneak preview of Peril on the Ranch *by Lynette Eason, available July 2021 from Love Inspired Suspense.*

Isabelle Trent woke with a start. She lay still, trying to figure out what had jarred her just as the sun was beginning to make its way above the horizon. She'd forgotten to pull her curtains closed before she'd fallen into bed with a half-finished prayer on her lips.

Maybe it was just the light that had disturbed her.

A faint cry reached her. A cry that sounded like…a baby? A kitten?

The sound grew louder, and it came from the wraparound porch.

Finally, she identified it.

A baby.

With a soft gasp, Isabelle hurried forward to unlock the French door and step outside.

At her feet, an infant was strapped into a carrier. "Oh, my sweet little one." Isabelle released the straps and scooped the tiny body, blanket and all, into her arms.

LISEXP0621